THE PRINCE
in WAITING

By John Christopher

THE
PRINCE
IN WAITING

by John Christopher

The Macmillan Company

TO ROSEMARY,
IN LIEU OF H. OR M.

CONTENTS

THE PRINCE
IN WAITING

ONE

Four Swords in Candlelight

The Armorer's forge was east of the river, in that part of the city called Chesil. It was a large, cavernous building, its floor of ancient stone cracked in places but all of a piece, dark except where the great central fire sent sparks springing up toward the square hole in the timbered roof. In the dimness the dwarfs moved here and there to the clang of metal on metal. They did not look up from their work when I came in. I stood for a moment by the door, watching and accustoming my eyes to the light. The Armorer Dwarf was on the far side of the fire, stooped over the big anvil. I went to stand beside him.

"Health, Rudi," I said.

He did not answer at once. He took a sword off the anvil and held it between himself and the fire, lifting it up and down slightly to judge its trueness by the shifting gleam of light. He nodded and gave it to the dwarf who stood beside him, balancing the blade on his palm and offering the hilt. Then he turned to me.

"Health, Master Luke. How is the world outside? Freezing yet? Your cheeks look as though frost has stroked them."

"It's cold enough. A north wind still."

"A pot of mulled ale, would you say?" He called an order to a dwarf apprentice who went off roll-gaited into the shadows. "Come and sit with me, Master Luke, and tell me how life goes in the city."

My eyes followed the sword which had been taken to the whetstone. The dwarf there treadled with his foot and the wheel went round. He brought the steel edge to it and bright sparks flew.

"Is that . . .?"

"For the Contest? No, those are already made and burnished. Would you see them?"

He lit a candle, thrusting the wick into the fire's heat in a way that would have scorched my flesh, and took it to the wall where swords hung waiting collection. The four made for the Contest rested apart from the others. They were also smaller, no more than two and a half feet from hilt to tip. Rudi took one down and handed it to me. The hilt fitted my grasp. I swung it lightly in the air.

Rudi watched me. He was big for a dwarf, close on five feet in height, and he did not have their squatness of figure to so marked an extent as was usual. His arms were brawny, muscled from his work, but the lower part of his body might almost have been human. His face was broad, brown and wrinkled, his hair and beard white. He said:

"Being chosen for the Contest is not everything, Master Luke."

I did not answer but swung the sword once more and gave it back. He hung it carefully on its hook.

They were not, of course, the swords that would actually be used in the Contest. Those were of wood, unpointed, capable of prodding or sweeping an opponent off his horse but not of penetrating the stiff leather jerkins they wore. But at the Contest's end each of the Young Captains would be given his real sword, one of these four. That nearest me had a red stone in its crosspiece that winked in the candlelight. It would go to the winner of the Contest, the conqueror.

Pots of ale were brought to us. Rudi offered me his own seat, its high back carved with the figures of past Armorers, but I refused it. I sat on a stool and sipped from the pewter pot. The ale was hot and sweet, flavored with spices. It warmed my throat and belly but did not lift the black depression from my shoulders.

Rudi said: "You would have been young for it."

"No younger than Matthew is."

"But his father is cousin to the Prince."

"Yes."

He drank deeply and gave his pot to a dwarf for refilling. He wiped the back of his hand across his mouth. "You take things hard, Master Luke. It is a failing, if I may presume to say so."

I would not have taken such a criticism from any other dwarf, but no other would have made it. In the past I had often taken troubles to Rudi and had good counsel from him. This counsel, too, might be good, but I got no comfort from it.

The Contest was part of the Fair which, in mid-March, was meant to mark the end of winter's grip, the coming of spring. (Though year by year, it seemed, the cold stayed longer, the trees were slower in budding.) In it four sons of Captains led their troops against one another in a series of skirmishes on the Contest Field. To be chosen one must be between thirteen and fourteen years of age. My thirteenth birthday had fallen two months ago.

This year three of the four contenders were obvious choices. There was Edmund, the Prince's second son. There was Henry, whose father, Captain Blaine, stood high in the Prince's war council. There was also Gregory, son of Captain Harding, and the Hardings ranked with the Blaines in distinction. And not only rank was in their favor. They were older than I—Henry would be fourteen a week after the Fair—and known to be good fighters. Matthew, on the other hand, was three weeks my junior and I could beat him any day at swordplay or jousting. But his father, as Rudi had said, was a cousin to the Prince while mine had been a Sergeant ennobled on the field of battle, a commoner born. My hopes of taking the fourth place had always been slim, but they had been hopes. And dashed three days ago when the herald cried the news at the palace gate. Matthew was to be the fourth Young Captain, and wear the sword afterward.

Rudi said: "It is not much help to tell anyone that he must bear his disappointments, but it is a truth that has to be learned. Some find it more difficult than others." His pot was returned brimming and he drank. "So they must school themselves harder."

"You can say that," I said, "as Master Armorer."

He nodded. "Master Armorer. And dwarf."

"But . . ."

I stopped. His words had startled me. If he had been a polymuf I might have understood. They, after all, were the lowest of the low, servants to men, landless, holding no property except at a master's whim. These things, as much as their deformities, set them apart, and while many fawned, some glowered. Disgusting to men, their condition must be hateful to themselves.

But dwarfs had pride, not just in their crafts but as a race. For the most part they bred true and could trace their families back for generations, often further than proper men. They had houses, small-holdings, polymuf servants. They could amass wealth and loved to dress their dumpy womenfolk in silks and decorate them with bright jewelry and heavy gold chains. They could not bear arms and so could not be ennobled, but they were, and knew themselves to be, essential to the life of the city as workers in metal and leather, weavers, brewers, grooms to the stables —all kind of necessary crafts. They could rise to positions of high status. Rudi himself had a seat at state banquets: below the second salt but at the Prince's table.

He said: "Even though you do not lead a troop at the Contest, next year you will be squired. In time you will be a Captain like your father."

"Rudi," I said, "would you have wished to be a warrior?"

I still could not believe it. I had heard dwarfs talk, and never known such a thing even hinted. They saw their kind as the builders and producers of the city's wealth, war as a sickness that afflicted proper men, laying waste to the land's prosperity. I had heard one say once that if there were only dwarfs all cities would be at peace and grow rich.

Rudi finished his second pot and laughed.

"A warrior, Master Luke? When I am Master Armorer? And will die at last in my bed, with no scars on my body except the small scars of my trade. But you would find it hard, I think, to make swords for other men to use. There are disappointments in all men's lives, even those who have achieved their ambition, and there are compensations. You are young and strong, and gaining skill in arms. You will go far in the Prince's service, and prosper. Not to be chosen for the Contest is a small thing to bear."

It was true, I supposed, but it did not help. I looked past him at the four swords on the wall, only dimly visible among the shadows that moved as the fire rose and fell with the blowing of the bellows. I had worn one of them in imagination all winter, sometimes the one with the red stone winking in its crosspiece. I had rejected that particular part of the daydream as futile, but the other had seemed possible. Having to abandon it was bitter.

Rudi threw his pot to the assistant dwarf and stood up.

"There is work still to do," he said. "Come, and I will show you how to put an edge on steel, in case a fairy touches you in the night and your legs shorten."

When I left the forge I crossed the river. There was confusion on the bridge, with carts jammed together and men shouting angrily, smoking the chill air with their curses. An overloaded cart had overturned and the way was blocked. The river, pouring violently from the millstream, ran free and turbulent at its center but the verges were rimmed with ice and downstream, between the grazing meadows, the ice spread right across from side to side. Farther down still it was thick enough for skating; or had been yesterday, and there could be no thaw with this sharp wind. I meant to go there in the afternoon but the morning had worn away and my chief thought was of dinner.

My home lay higher up in the city, among the houses that surrounded the Prince's palace. I did not go that way, though, but turned right along the street that ran parallel with the river for a while, and was called the River Road. The house into which I went was small but well kept, shutters and door painted bright blue, window sills and flagstones underneath them scoured and whitened. Bedding hung from the open windows at the top and would do so until mid-afternoon, when mattresses, sheets, blankets and eiderdowns were taken in for the beds to be made up and heated with the wrapped bricks that now lay at the back of the hearth. Everything was spick and span and in good order. This was my Aunt Mary's house.

She was not truly my aunt, but my father's first wife. They had known each other as children and he had married her when he was a young warrior. They had a son, my half brother Peter, whom I called cousin. Riding to war with the Prince (the old Prince, our present Prince's father) my father had seen a farmer's daughter, my mother, whose beauty had amazed and confounded him. It was in that campaign that he was made Captain and so could divorce his wife, on petition to the Prince, and take another. He divorced my Aunt Mary and brought his young bride back to the city, and the next year I was born.

He had made provision for his first wife and child. He would have done so even if the law had not required it because he was a just man. Moreover, although he no longer loved her, he respected my Aunt Mary and came to her house often, not just to see his son but to talk to her and listen to her advice. And I, from my earliest days of roaming abroad, treated her house as my second home.

In some ways, even, I preferred it to my own. It was smaller, pokier, but clean and sweet smelling. My aunt had only two polymuf servants, my mother eight or nine, but the two were closely watched and supervised, the eight or nine for the most part slack and grumbling. From time to time my mother, in despair, would have my father dismiss one or more and get others, hiding in her room while this was done, and would make resolutions that in the future everything would be different. It never was. I heard my father say one day in exasperation that no one could have imagined such a thing—a farmer's daughter who knew less of running a house than a lady of five generations' idleness. She wept, and he forgot his annoyance in comforting her.

She was beautiful. At thirty she had the skin, the face and figure of a girl. Her likeness hung on the walls of half a dozen great houses, including the palace itself: Margry, the Prince's painter, had had her sit for him a score of times. And yet she aroused no spite or jealousy among the ladies of the court. Everyone recognized she was without malice and therefore she provoked none. I had seen her petulant sometimes but never angry. For the most part she was happy, talkative, eager to please and to be pleased. She liked sunshine and pet animals and glancing at her own beauty in the glass.

My Aunt Mary was very different. She was gray-haired and had a long harsh face scored with years of work and brooding. She was deep-natured. She did not make a show of her feelings—she spoke little and smiled less—but their strength was shown in small things: a brief condemnation of that person, a rare word of praise for this. Of all men she most respected my father and continued to treat him as master of the house which he had left when he divorced her. Toward others, with a single exception, she was reserved. That one was her son, my cousin Peter. Him she loved with the depth and fierceness of a river forced to run between narrow banks. Even this she strove to hide, but it could not be hidden.

She would have accepted me because of my father—it was his house and his son, though by another wife, must be made welcome in it—but I fancied she liked me a little apart from that. She was strict, as she was in everything, and I would never have dared to go to her table with unwashed hands as I had sometimes done at home. But she showed me some kindness, and somehow my black moods sat on me less heavily in her house. It was not that she indulged me in them, if anything the reverse, but that my misery seemed less important in the presence of her watchful austerity.

This morning she greeted me with a nod and told me that dinner was almost ready. I had scented it, a stew whose rich smell made my appetite clamorous. At home the polymuf cook used the best of meats and vegetables but the stews were thin and tasteless. I went to the kitchen to wash and saw one of the polymufs scouring a pan. (My aunt did her own cooking but kept her servants busy with cleaning and polishing.) This was Gerda; she had short arms and the mark of an extra eye on her forehead, though it had never opened. She bobbed her head to me without ceasing her work. My aunt allowed her servants fair periods of rest but required good labor the rest of the time.

I was at the table and eating when Peter came in. I heard him tethering his horse outside and he pulled off his big leather coat as he entered. Gerda brought a bowl of hot water, soap and a towel, and he washed in the hall as befitted a grown man. He was eighteen, a Sergeant under my father's command, soon to be made Mister as the junior Captains were called. When he had finished he took the seat at the head of the table, which was his except when my father dined here. He said to me cheerfully:

"Have you heard the news, Luke?"

"What news?"

"Matthew Grant went skating this morning and broke a leg."

I looked up quickly and saw him laughing. I flushed and turned back to my dinner, for which, suddenly, my appetite had gone. Aunt Mary said:

"Do not tease him."

Peter said: "You are not brooding over this, Luke, are you? You would have had no chance of lasting beyond the first round. You would have been cut down in a few minutes and earned nothing but jeers."

He had seen that the jest had hurt me and was doing his best to put things right. I knew he would not wound me except by accident. He was slow-moving and amiable, a smiling contrast to his mother's dourness. Not slow in thought; his mind was sharp enough. Except where people were concerned. There he did not look below the surface, accepting them as they were or as they seemed to be.

In appearance he was tall, broad-shouldered, fair, resembling my father much more than I did. I was of no more than average height, stockier, swarthy in my looks. I suppose I was more like my aunt, who was no blood kin to me, than either of my parents. Peter, like my mother, had no enemies, and for much the same reason. But unlike her he was warm in his affections. He went on talking, saying too much was made of the Contest. He had not been chosen and what difference had it made? Digby, who won the jewel in that year, was giving up soldiering to marry a merchant's daughter and turn shopkeeper.

What he did not understand was that I was different from both him and Digby. It had not mattered that he had not got a place because he had not minded, but I did. It only made it the more bitter that someone like Digby, willing now to give up being a warrior, should have had the chance to win the jeweled sword. If Peter did not resent it, he ought to.

But he soothed me enough for the smell of Aunt Mary's stew to tempt me back into hunger and I ate my dinner. There was apple pie to follow, made from apples picked in the autumn, then peeled and ringed and hung to dry on long lines in the attic. Afterward we sat in front of the fire in the living room until the clock on the mantel struck two. At that Peter yawned and stretched and stood up, his fair head almost touching the low whitewashed ceiling.

"Time to be back. More formation training. I think we must be the best formation riders this side of the Burning Lands. We may not fight, but we ride very well."

He spoke in jest but there were others who said much the same and more sourly. The city had been five years at peace and men were restless.

In this we had separated ourselves from the customs of

the civilized lands. The summer campaigns were a part of the pattern of living, as much as the feasts of spring and autumn and mid-winter. In the yearly challenge to its enemies a city maintained its pride, and through pride purpose. This was, moreover, the source of all honor. The dwarfs might be content with their crafts and trades, but for a proper man in his youth and strength the only true glory lay in fighting for his city. If he was killed his body was brought back to lie with the other heroes in the Citadel; if he was crippled his Prince cared for him as long as he lived. And if, as was more often the case, he returned unscathed or with minor wounds he had his fame; and stories to tell, boasts to make during the long idleness of winter.

The Prince's father, Egbert, had been a great fighter; it was under him that my own father had been ennobled in a savage battle against the men of Basingstoke. Our new Prince was very different. Each year he found some reason for not taking our army into the field. From the beginning there had been doubts of his valor and the doubts had grown as summer succeeded summer with fresh excuses. He was a big man with a black curling beard but had a strangely empty look, like a vessel that had missed being filled.

There was a tale which had never been forgotten of a wrestling contest when he was a young man. It was that form of wrestling in which the object is not to throw one's opponent to the ground but to lift him off his feet and hold him in the air. Stephen, though even then big for his age, had chosen the smallest of the group to contend against, presumably because he doubted his chances with the others. And after a great struggle this one, though inches shorter and narrow of chest, had lifted him not once but twice, the second time carrying him helpless round the ring.

So his excuses now—an illness of his Lady, the weather being unpropitious or the crops needing special attention, once a warning from the Spirits in a dream (he said) of disaster to the city if the troops went forth—were suspect. Last year he was supposed to have injured his back, so that he could not ride or even walk without pain, and he had kept to his bed for two months. But it had been remarked that he walked well enough when the Autumn Feast came round, and rode to the Hunt afterward.

And all this time the reputation which his father had gained, for himself and for the city, was dissipating. It did not happen at once: our warriors had made themselves feared and respected as far afield as Guildford and Newbury and Ringwood, and our neighbors were glad enough at first to be free of their attentions. But lately it was known that they had begun to mock him and us. Last year the men of Alton had ridden into our lands while Stephen lay on his bed, with blocks of wood tied to his feet to straighten out the kink he was supposed to have in his spine, and carried away more than four score head of cattle. It was important that this year we should go after them and teach them a lesson, but no one really believed that our Prince would move. Year after year he had built the city's walls higher and deepened the ditch beyond them.

Aunt Mary said: "There is no sense in fighting for the sake of fighting. They wound and kill each other and are no better for it."

Peter shook his head. "That is the way a woman thinks."

He smiled and put a hand on her shoulder. She impatiently shook herself free; she would not admit how much she welcomed the signs of his affection.

"It is not a question of men or women," she said. "I am not against fighting—or killing—if it is for something worthwhile. But not for empty glories, paid for with real deaths."

Peter smiled past her at me. What she said meant nothing to him, nor would it have to any warrior. A man fought for the sake of fighting, for his own honor and the honor of his city. Accepting the complicity he offered me, proud of being spoken to as someone who would one day be a warrior and understood the way a warrior thought, I said:

"I wonder how our Prince will get out of it this year. Maybe he will have them take him into Sincross!"

Sincross was the big house in which the old men lived whose wits had failed through age. It was a feeble enough joke at best but as I saw Peter frown I remembered something. Younger people also were taken there when the Spirits had crazed their brains. This had been the case with Aunt Mary's brother many years ago, even before Peter's birth, and he had died in madness when not much more than twenty. And I remembered too that I had heard talk once, among servants who did not realize I was listening, that it had been thought the same might happen to Aunt

Mary herself at the time my father divorced her, so strange she had been and so deeply sunk in melancholy.

I was struck into confusion by my thoughtlessness and could not look at Aunt Mary. But she seemed anyway to pay no heed to my remark. She was concerned with Peter, with making sure that he put on his scarf and wound it tight around his body under his leather coat before going out into the cold. As a child, she reminded him, scolding gently, he had had a weakness in his chest and he must take care.

I left with him and watched him unhitch his horse. Peter's frown had gone. He offered to ride me up the hill on his saddlebow but I refused. I might not have been chosen for the Contest but I felt I was too old for that. Until I had a horse of my own, I would walk.

Before I could go skating I had to go home and get my skates and so I made my way up the High Street rather than along the river bank. It was a little less cold, or perhaps seemed so because my stomach was full. In a few places, missed by the polymuf street cleaners, snow lay in frozen, dirt-specked ridges. The last fall had been a week ago. The sky was hazy with a watery sun peering through. Winter's grip seemed as firm as ever. Carts creaked past me, one of them piled high with fodder. I had heard my father say that supplies were very low and grain too in short supply. There would be more cattle slaughtered unless the cold spell broke soon, and probably some horses.

My name was called from behind. I knew the voice and

involuntarily shivered. I turned and saw Ezzard striding toward me, his black cloak wrapped tightly round his tall lean frame. I waited for him to come up, telling myself I was no longer a child to be frightened by the Seer. His Spirits did not venture out of the Seance Hall, and anyway I had done nothing to offend them.

But he was a man who in himself inspired awe. Taller even than my father, he had a craggy face with a beaked nose and black bushy eyebrows. His eyes were set deep and close together and were cold and blue. His skin was very white, as though he spent all his time in darkness and not just the hours when he was communing with the Spirits. In the summer when the light was stronger he wore spectacles that were darkly tinted; even without these there seemed a strange blankness, an emptiness, in his look.

He said: "Where are you bound, boy?"

I did not care for being addressed as "boy," and even though it was the Seer I answered a little stiffly. But his eyes, staring into mine, made me drop my gaze.

He said: "You respect the Spirits?"

"Yes, sire."

"There are some, of your age, who do not—who mock foolishly."

I said: "I have seen the Spirits and heard them."

He nodded. "Remember that. Remember another thing: that the Spirits take care of those who show them proper reverence. The fools who mock at last are mocked. And they are fools all along."

"Yes, sire."

He raised his hand in the blessing, though as Ezzard gave it it was almost menacing.

"Away to your skating, then. Make the most of it. It will be your last of the winter."

I did not need to seek a meaning to that riddle. The Spirits foretold the weather to him. The thaw was coming and by tomorrow the ice would be too weak to bear. I was flattered that he should have told me this, as though I were one of the Prince's messengers. I nodded and turned to go. As I did his hand grasped my shoulder.

"Perhaps your last indeed."

I shivered again. One skated until one became a man, and one was not a man until fifteen. There were times when the Spirits prophesied a death.

But he was smiling, his face improbably drawn into a grin.

"Go your way, Luke. The Spirits go with you."

I found Martin and we took our skates to the river. In the morning he had been busy with duties; his mother was a widow and too poor to afford even a single polymuf servant. We skated for a couple of hours and by the end of that time one could tell the change that was taking place: the wind had swung from north to west and there was mildness in it. I told him of Ezzard's words as we walked back. He said:

"He is right often enough. But how?"

"Through the Spirits. How else?"

"But how?"

Martin was not even as tall as I, and slim with it. He had a girl's skin, delicate, almost transparent, and his brown eyes were big like a girl's. We had become friends when I rescued him from other boys who were tormenting him. The biggest of them was someone I very much disliked, and it was more through this than through a desire to help Martin that I had taken him on and given him a beating. It was only later that I grew to like Martin. His mind was curious, odd in its way of thinking, restless and speculative. Sometimes absurdly so. I said:

"The Spirits know the future as they know the past. And they tell Ezzard because he is the Seer. There is nothing difficult about it."

He did not answer, and we did not pursue the matter because there was a horseman riding toward us, along Burnt Lane. I recognized horse and rider. My father called:

"Greetings, son! I was told you were down at the river and I came out to meet you."

His lips laughed between the fair beard and curling yellow moustache. He would not have done this for a trivial reason. My heart leaped, but I said as evenly as I could:

"What news, sir?"

"Young Grant is ill. A fever. He will not fight on Thursday. You have his place in the Contest."

I stared at him. He leaned down and swept me onto his saddlebow, and I did not resent it. We rode homeward, Martin running beside us.

And I thought of what Ezzard had said. A Young Captain was called a man, though not fifteen. I would not skate next winter with the boys, but serve the Prince as apprentice warrior. There had been two prophecies after all.

TWO

THE YOUNG
CAPTAINS

We had a day to prepare for the Contest and it rained almost continually. It was a cold drizzle to start with, soaking and depressing, and after a couple of hours of slithering and sliding and falling on the practice field Edmund called his team together and rode them off. Henry and Gregory followed suit. To have continued after the Prince's son had stopped would have been to risk being mocked at for too great keenness, and I think in any case they were glad enough to head for home.

I brought my own team off the field but set a slow pace along the road to the city, and by the time we reached the fork at the Elder Pond the others, galloping toward a change of clothes, hot drinks and warm fires, were out of sight. At the pond I called them to take the left fork, away from the city. They halted in confusion. I reined in and rode slowly back.

Laurie, who was the best man I had, said:

"Why left?"

I waited, letting them look at me, for some moments before replying. I said:

"Listen. I am your Captain. We are the weakest team in the Contest. Do you know the odds they are offering in the alehouses against our winning? Fifty to one, and I have heard that some have offered a hundred without finding takers."

They stared at me, drenched and miserable, the flanks of their horses steaming. An unprepossessing lot even without being bedraggled and spotted with mud.

The number of each team in the Contest was fixed at four, apart from the Junior Captain. It would have been fairer if selection had been by lot but the test was as much as anything for leadership and a leader chooses his men. Or is chosen by them. Of those who, being of the age and yet not of noble family, could take part, most naturally would have preferred to follow the Prince's son. Not for the honor only, of course: he was favored to win and the winning team, to match their Captain's jeweled sword, drew gold coins as a reward. The teams coming second and third obtained silver and bronze, while that which was first eliminated got nothing but the mob's derision for its pains.

Because of this I had been left with, for the most part, those already rejected by the other leaders. Martin, of course, had volunteered at once. He was not a good horseman and was a poorer swordsman but at least I knew he would fight hard for me. And there was some consolation, too, as far as the rest were concerned, in thinking that they were willing to take part with so little prospect of victory or reward. Even if lacking in skill they were eager for the fight.

I said: "They believe we are certain to lose. But nothing is certain, neither victory nor defeat. Skill counts for much, but so does preparation and hard work. The others have gone home. Soon they will be stabling their horses and taking things easy. We may be weaker in some respects but we can be stronger in endurance. We are not going back to the city but to a quiet place where we can train undisturbed and unobserved. You are wet and tired. So am I. We cannot get wetter and if we get more tired we shall sleep the better tonight and be more refreshed for tomorrow. Laurie!"

"Yes, Captain."

That was good. He was supposed to give me the title but I had thought I might have to demand it. I said, still harshly:

"You asked: 'Why left?' From now on, in training first and then in the fight, none puts such a question to me. Is that clear?" My eyes went from one to the other, forcing them to nod assent. "I give commands. You obey. If this is done well enough, I shall wear the jeweled sword tomorrow, and you will have gold." I turned my horse from them and from the road to the city. "Follow."

What I had been telling them was, I was sure, nonsense,

at any rate insofar as any hopes of our winning the Contest were concerned. What I really wanted was to avoid coming last. As I have said, the team first eliminated always drew jeers from the crowd and I could not bear the thought of it. If we could survive into the second round, I would be happy enough. I had two reasons for pitching things high to my men. One was to shatter the pessimism they must feel over our chances; the second to give them heart for the grueling task ahead, because I meant to keep them at it till both we and our horses were ready to drop from exhaustion. I would risk them going tired into the fight. I was determined we should go in more ready for the tricks our opponents might play, more skilled in evading or countering them.

My father had the lordship of a farm a few miles from the eastern gate. I had the farmer get his polymufs to drive cattle from a field and we went at it there. In the Contest, as in all fighting on horseback, understanding and control of one's horse comes first. The horses we had were drawn from the army stables and their ways needed learning. To get mounts for their troop the Young Captains drew lots and chose in turn. The others had gone, as was usual, for the bigger horses. I had let them do so; the ground would be heavy after rain. From one of the grooms, a dwarf I knew well, I sought advice as to which of the smaller beasts were best for stamina, speed, sure-footedness, and I picked them. I had already found that he had given me good guidance. The horses were sound; now it was up to me and my men to learn to handle them. I split the men in two pairs, myself taking first one side then the other, and we rode at each other in mock battle.

The aim of each team must be to unsaddle the opposing Captains, because once the Captain is dismounted that team retires. There are scores, hundreds, of different tactics which can be employed, but nearly all revolve around a situation in which the Captain has two defending outriders and two attacking ones. This, I had decided, must be abandoned for a start. I could not afford to hide behind defenders, even if the defense were reliable. My only hope lay in deliberately taking chances.

In close fighting there were countless forms of assault and parry. The wooden swords were our offensive weapons, and we carried small leather shields as a means of defense, but by getting in close enough one could buffet or drag a man from his horse, or pluck, swooping, at his stirrup and upend him. I had studied tricks of Captains in previous years, and there were one or two of my own that I added. I rehearsed my men (and myself) in these over and over again. Beyond that we practiced riding in various patterns and directions in response to signals of command. It was a slow business and more often than not ended in confusion and disorder.

After another couple of hours, I ordered a break. The farmer had prepared food and drink for us and they were more than ready for it, but first I saw to it that the ponies were fed and watered and rubbed down and blanketed. We ate heartily and I let the men rest a while afterward. Then I called them back to work. They groaned but made no protest. The rain was still soaking down, as steadily though perhaps less chilly. We slogged on as the afternoon drew slowly toward dusk. The sky's gray was tinged with black when at last I gave the order to break off. We rode back slowly, dog-tired, to the city.

I swore them to secrecy before we parted; if anyone asked, we had spent the day in the farmhouse, penned in by the rain, gambling with dice. Of the dwarf groom, Murri, I asked the same confidence. Seeing to the ponies with me, he said:

"You could have lamed them, Master."

"But did not." I gave him money. "A good bran mash tonight, with strong ale in it, and tomorrow the best oats you can find. They will be all right for the afternoon?"

"They will be all right." He looked up at me, grinning. "I will cheer for you, Master Luke."

"Will you back me?"

"No." He wagged his broad head. "We dwarfs are men of heart, as is well known, but we do not let our hearts rule our minds. And we are no believers in miracles."

I nodded. I think I was too tired to smile.

It was my intention to slip quietly into my home and get the servants to fill me a bath. But as I crossed the court-yard my father called from his window and I had to go to him. He said:

"Where have you been, Luke? The others were back by mid-morning."

"We went out to the farm, sir. Cooper gave us food."

"You stayed the whole day there?"

"It was raining. There seemed small point in coming back."

"Doing what?"

"Dicing. And talking. Idling, I suppose."

He looked at me through the open window. "Was that the best way you could find of passing the time on the day before the Contest?"

"I am sorry, sir."

"You are a strange lad. You keep your own counsel, even from me." I waited. The lamp was behind him but I saw him smile. "You cannot see yourself, can you? Or smell yourself. If you roll in muck long enough your nose grows accustomed to it. You are covered not just in mud but cow-dung. Did you dice out in the fields, in the wet? And has idling bowed your shoulders?"

"Sir . . ."

He cut across my words. "I will not keep you in the rain. But listen to one thing. It is proper to be ambitious but do not overreach yourself. Yesterday you had been passed over for the Contest. Today you are one of the four Young Captains and tomorrow you will ride out with your men to the Field. I only ask that you acquit yourself well. Do not hope for too much and risk the bitterness of disappointment. You know how it takes you."

"I will do as you say, sir."

The smile had gone. He stared at me a while longer, then said:

"Get yourself washed and changed. We will meet at supper."

He closed the window and turned away.

I awoke in the small hours of the night, the sweat chilling on my exposed flesh where, in my dream, I had pushed the covers back. The dream was with me still, and vivid. I was alone on a vast field, far greater than the Contest Field, and my enemies were chasing me. I had no help, no hope and no courage to do the one thing I knew I must do: turn and face them. They overhauled but did not quite take me and I knew that this was because they did not wish to yet, because they were playing with me, cats with a terrified mouse. All round and it seemed from the sky above came the mocking roar of the crowd, urging on my enemies, laughing me to scorn.

I lay there, sweating and trembling, and then got up. I fumbled in the dark for my pitcher of water, and drank. Then I went to the windows and pulled them open. The rain had stopped and the night was very still, black except for the glow behind the western hills that marked the Burning Lands. A dog barked far off, once and no more.

It had been a nightmare, a vexation, as Ezzard would have told me, of the unguarded mind by those Spirits who ruled the domain of sleep. I had eaten too richly the night before—in my hunger I had devoured half a loaf of bread and a huge chunk of cheese. Apart from that I could pay a penny to the Acolyte, to ask the Spirits who protected men to give me special care. And now I must dismiss it from my mind, go back to bed, sleep and be refreshed for tomorrow.

I returned to my bed but I did not sleep. Thoughts ran jumbled through my head, not about the dream but the reality. I imagined the fight, looked at it from every point of view, and from every point of view was driven to the same conclusion: we had no chance at all. It was a standard operation for the three stronger teams to concentrate first on eliminating the weakest. I had worked out plans to counter this but here in the still center of the night I recognized their futility. They would only, as I saw, expose us to greater mockery when they failed.

I thought of my father's warning and acknowledged the truth of it. Pride and ambition ran too strongly in me. It would be better to settle for what I had, to be contented with my lot. It was, after all, a good one. I had been born true man, not dwarf nor, God forbid, polymuf. I had been born in this city of a noble father—of no lineage, but noble. I had my health and strength, the use of my wits. Now, by the fortune of another's falling sick, I was chosen a Junior Captain and, whatever happened in the Contest, would wear a sword tomorrow night at the feast. Even if we were ignominiously defeated, I myself unhorsed in the first charge, the defeat and the derision that went with it, the hissing and the laughter, were a small price to pay for what I gained.

That was the sensible way to look at it. But as I thought

of the mob and its ridicule the sweat was cold again on my back and down my legs. I turned violently in my bed, striking the pillow with my fist, willing my mind to blankness, willing sleep to come. I must rest, to be strong for the day ahead. But the more I demanded, the further sleep drew from me. At last I turned to pleading. I called on the Spirits of my Ancestors to aid me. That, too, did not help. The window's square had begun to pale before exhaustion succeeded where demands and pleas had failed, and I slept.

Then the maid, Janet, was shaking my shoulder gently. It was broad day. I looked at her through eyes that would scarcely open, my mind fogged and stupid.

"Time to rise, Master Luke."

I asked: "What day is this?"

She smiled at me. She had no visible deformities but she wore her dresses high up at the neck. A good-looking woman but she was past thirty and had not married; though most polymufs did. The destructive Spirits, one guessed, had done their work cruelly on her.

"Contest Day, Master Luke," she said. "Your day."

It rained all morning but the rain was warm now. Blowing direct from the Burning Lands, it left a coating of gray behind it. I could imagine my Aunt Mary's lips tightening as she watched the white sills and flags outside her house besmirched. The polymufs would be hard at work as soon as the rain ceased.

And it did cease around midday. In the early afternoon the Young Captains rode their troops out of the city with leather jackets dry and silver epaulets gleaming in a watery sunlight. We rode in procession across the bridge and through the East Gate. The Prince and his Captains led the way, followed by their ladies. Next came Ezzard and the Acolytes; then the Young Captains in order of lineage. Edmund first, of course, as son of the Prince, followed by Gregory and Henry. I came last. After us the senior burgesses, the Sergeants, farmers in for the day. Then the common people, then the dwarfs. Last of all the polymufs. There was chattering and laughter, and strollers playing instruments and singing songs.

The city would be almost emptied of people, the walls which Prince Stephen had built so high stood unmanned. It was true that this was the time of the Spring Fair when no war was made throughout the civilized lands. The Spirits forbade it. But if someone broke the truce, I wondered, did that mean the Spirits would defend the city lying at the attacker's mercy? Their ways, as even the Seers admitted, were capricious; neither punishment nor reward was certain. I remembered my own desperate pleas for sleep and how they had gone unanswered. Contests like this one were held in the other cities, too. Romsey, for instance, no more than ten miles to the southwest . . . a handful of men, riding swiftly, could take and hold it.

I dismissed the speculations as futile. It was the custom to keep peace until after the Spring Fair. Even to think of anything different was to offend the Spirits. They had not helped me in the night but they might still help me in the fight to come. And I needed help, all the help I could get.

We came to the Contest Field and Ezzard blessed the contestants in the name of the Spirits. Tents had been erected at one end for the nobles. I saw my father and mother there, and Peter. Not Aunt Mary. A woman who married a nobleman became a lady but the wife he had put aside had no rank. I trotted my horse past the throngs of commoners and found her, wedged in at the front. I dismounted and bowed to her.

"Greetings, Aunt Mary. Wish me well."

She nodded fiercely. "I do that, Luke."

A man nearby made a jest about my chances and others laughed. She turned on them and they fell silent. I mounted and rode to where my parents sat. My mother said:

"Don't get hurt."

She spoke in a little frightened voice. She had clapped her hands with delight on hearing that I had been picked to be a Young Captain. She lived in the moment. Nothing was real to her before it happened, or mattered much after.

My father said: "I know you will fight hard, so I have nothing to tell you. The Spirits go with you."

The first gong boomed and it was time to bow our heads before the Prince. On the second gong the Contest started.

Each Captain took a corner of the field. I had the western one, nearest to the city but farthest from the Prince's tent. I waited with my men and spoke to them quietly:

"Remember, keep silence."

It was usual for the teams to go into the fight noisily,

yelling threats and imprecations. To cause fear, I suppose. It seemed to me that if mine were not already frightened by the odds against them a few shouts would not make them so. Our keeping silence would set us apart from the others but perhaps not to our disadvantage. It would also, I felt, help us to concentrate more, and help my men more easily listen to my commands.

The second gong boomed.

The four teams advanced warily from their corners. There were a number of ways in which a Contest might begin. Sometimes the teams circled the field for a period, keeping their distances, until one broke into an assault on another. Sometimes they met right away in a furious all-in melee toward the center. There was another possibility which I had dreaded, and my heart sank as I realized that this was what was happening. The other three teams were converging on ours; they were combining to eliminate the weakest before settling down to a Contest of three.

I had made my plan and I was committed to it. If it did not come off it must make me look a fool or a coward, more probably both. The distances narrowed and I waited for the moment and watched for the opening. It must be left till the very last instant but the last instant could be too late. They had started hurling threats and catcalls at us. I said to Laurie on my left:

"Stand when I break. After that, it's up to you."

They were not hurrying. Edmund's troop were a little ahead of the rest and I saw him rein in to let the other two come up. They were out to crush us completely and were taking no chances. They were within twenty feet, fifteen. The best gap was between Henry's troop and the fence. Sharply I dug in spurs and set my pony's head toward it.

The roar from the crowd momentarily drowned the yells of our attackers. As I have said, a team was eliminated as soon as its Captain was unhorsed. To bolt away from the protection of one's men was unheard of. My team, I knew, were standing fast behind me. Out of the corner of my eye I saw the other teams confusedly trying to change direction. My sudden move had taken them by surprise but they were rallying to follow the obvious quarry. They must think me mad or panic-stricken. Whichever it was their aim remained the same and its fulfillment now was easier. They were certain of riding me down.

One of Henry's men swiped at me but did not reach me as I got through the gap. I eased off, not to put too great a distance between me and my pursuers, and rode not for the corner diagonally opposite but for the nearer north corner. The field was a big one, of more than a hundred acres, but it seemed small to me now. Fortunately they did not have the sense to fan out but came after me in a bunch. Fifteen yards from the corner I wheeled and made my second dash, past their left flank.

I did not clear it fully this time. Two got glancing blows in on me and ahead I saw an outrider. I had to go between him and his nearest companion and they moved as I did, to sandwich me. They almost succeeded. My horse squealed as the shoulder of a big bay slammed against her rump, and a chopping blow from a sword made my head ring and rocked me in the saddle. But they could not hold me. I was through again and this time heard the cry I had been waiting for, Laurie's exultant shout:

"Three down! Against Gregory!"

This had been my plan. I had gambled that, in hot expectant pursuit of me, they would ignore my team. These, under Laurie's command, had ridden in chase of the chasers, with the aim of picking off men in that team which was straggler to the others. And the ruse had succeeded: they had got three of Gregory's men before anyone realized what was happening. Now as I wheeled once more they rode back to me in triumph while the rest, confused again and uncertain, rallied to their own Captains.

The uncertainty did not last long. We were no longer the weakest, to be harried and destroyed. Three of Gregory's men were limping from the field, their horses running free. Gregory, with his last remaining follower, backed toward the north corner. He knew what must follow.

The three teams came in on him for the kill, but here again our intention was not what it seemed. We left the unhorsing of Gregory to the others, going ourselves for Henry. Laurie and I pulled down one of his men while the other three got a second. Then I rode for Henry himself. My sword crashed against his shield. In riposte he got through my defense and struck me in the ribs, jerking me backward. I was struggling to keep my foot in the stirrups when the gong boomed to a new tumult from the crowd.

The first Captain was down, bringing the first interval. Henry and I drew away from each other and I saw Gregory walking disconsolately toward the Captains' tent.

The tactics of the second round were simpler. Edmund and I needed no conference to establish the advantages that lay for both of us in cooperation. Our teams were intact while Henry was reduced to a single man on either side. We must join forces to crush him.

But although the aim was simple it proved far from easy. Henry fought tigerishly and with intelligence, again and again forcing a way clear of us and gaining a breathing space. I lost Martin before either of Henry's two men were down. If I lost another we would be as weak as he was—weaker because he had better men—and things could turn against us. I shouted to Laurie and he and I picked out Henry's left flanker and attacked him together. He parried my blow but Laurie's, coming in from the other side, toppled him from the saddle.

Even then it was not over. When Henry was at last alone he fought on for what seemed an age, earning the crowd's acclaim. But we got him in the end, dragging him down almost, as hounds would a stag. The gong sounded and wearily we drew apart. Only then did I realize that two more men had gone, one from Edmund's team and the other, a lad called Carey, from my own.

We were all battered by this time and Laurie was streaming blood from a gash just below his ear. My head rang from the blows I had received, despite my leather helmet, and my shield arm was so stiff and painful that even raising the shield was an agony. (Two of the dismounted, we learned, had broken arms, a third a dislocated shoulder.) But we had survived two rounds, against odds. We had good reason to be proud. We could rest on the laurels we had already won. It would not matter if Edmund overwhelmed us at the end.

As, plainly, he must do. He had four men against three and the four were stronger and better fighters. There was no more room for tricks of playing one against another. Our horses were tired, too, their early nimbleness worn down by the pounding of the fight and the sticky churned-up mud of the field. We had done better than anyone could have guessed and though Edmund took the jeweled sword he would not take all the credit.

But although before the Contest I would have settled gladly for the present situation, now, fiercely, my ambition demanded more. In a battle of attrition we had no chance but if . . . I spoke to my two remaining followers. Laurie shook his head.

"It cannot succeed."

"Perhaps not. But neither can anything else."

The gong sounded again and we came out of our corners. Edmund and his men rode slowly, bunched together. On my command, though, my two swung left while I myself bore right. I saw Edmund halt his team, considering.

He was alert for tricks but he could not see one here. We, the weaker side, had split our forces and I, their Captain, was heading away from my men. His response did not need much working out. He detached two of his men toward my two, to hold them if they could not overcome them. He and his chief lieutenant, a huge brawny lad called Tom, headed for me.

They split as they drew near, to take me one on either side. I had expected that, too. Ten yards, five. I freed my feet from the stirrups. They came at me, swords raised to slash. As they did so, as Edmund's horse came alongside mine, I threw myself out of my saddle and onto him.

He could have withstood me if he had kept his head, but he flinched. I got him by the neck, dragging him down. Tom tried to get round to help him but could not do so for my horse. Edmund and I crashed to the ground together.

The rule had it that if the last two Captains were dismounted simultaneously they must remount and meet for a decision, but this time unassisted. I watched him ride toward me from his corner. I had thought my shield arm hurt before but now it felt as though a thousand devils were sitting on it, driving in claws of fire. He was stronger than I was and had beaten me often enough in swordplay. Under normal conditions I was no match for him in single combat.

But conditions were not normal. Twice that afternoon I had surprised him. In addition, I was Captain of a team the others had contemptuously decided to eliminate at the start and we had won through. And he had flinched when I fell on him, and he knew I knew it.

I had kept silence throughout the Contest. But as we closed I yelled deep in my throat, a yell of hate and triumph. I watched his eyes and saw them wince. Then there was no time for anything but fighting as our swords smacked heavily together. He held his ground for a few minutes and we traded blows. His horse was heavy enough to have forced mine back but he lacked the will for it. Instead it was he who gave way. I prodded his horse's flank with my sword. It reared and he fell, almost willingly.

Not looking back I rode my horse toward the Prince's tent.

tHREE

THE SEANCE
of tHE CROWNS

Two days after the end of the Spring Fair, the earth quaked. It happened in mid-morning and I was in the grazing meadows riding the horse my father had given me for my victory in the Contest. It was a roan gelding of fourteen hands and he knew of the quake before it happened, as was often the case with animals: he halted and whinnied with fear, and stood there shivering. As my foot touched the ground, dismounting, it seemed to move away from me, in a heavy rolling which made me stagger and almost fall.

I do not know how long the earth's shivering lasted—minutes, I thought, but probably I was deceived. To be without that firmness and solidity underfoot, which one takes for granted, even for ten seconds can seem an eternity.

I stayed holding the reins after the rolling stopped, the horse and I both quivering as though the quake were dying away in our nerve ends. But nothing more happened. Dogs which had been barking in the distance fell silent. The air was calm. I remounted my horse and rode into the city to see what damage there had been.

Not a great deal, as it happened. Three houses had collapsed; there were two dead and five or six injured. By the standards of those who remembered the old days it was very little. But because the earth had been quiet for so long—I could not recall such a thing though my father told me there had been several during the first few years of my life—there was fear that the evil times were returning. In the city I found people talking of sleeping out in the open that night, abandoning the city as they had done in the past, and some were already loading their goods on carts. A long line had formed outside the tent-seller's shop in the High Street and it was said he was asking twenty pounds for his smallest tents and finding eager buyers. The bakers had sold out of bread; all the food shops were besieged.

As the day wore by, though, with no more shocks, the panic died away. There were some who continued to move out of the city, but not many, and I saw others mocking them as cowards. Even if more quakes came the risk of staying was worth taking, provided they were no more severe than this. Our houses, after all, were built to withstand the smaller shiftings of the earth. (Our ancestors had built in stone and metal, their houses hundreds of feet high, and had died under the rubble of their tumbled pride.) Our houses were of wood and the beams so laid that they yielded one against another under pressure, but the structure itself remained intact.

In the afternoon a rumor spread which caused more alarm: that the Prince and his family were among those who were fleeing to open ground. Others were minded to follow suit and the streets began to be crowded again. Then my father and the other Captains rode out with troops of horsemen and branded the rumor as a lie: the Prince was in his palace and would remain there. The people should stay in their houses. Through Ezzard, the Spirits had advised this.

Before supper I was called to my father's room by Ben, the polymuf who waited on him. He was hunch-backed and had only two thickened fingers on his right hand, one of them showing two separate bones beneath the skin. I found my cousin Peter there already. They both looked grave.

My father said: "You are old enough now, Luke, to listen to warrior's business. But you know that, without my permission, you do not talk of things I have told you outside these walls." I nodded. "There is trouble in the city."

I waited. Peter said: "This may also be a rumor, Father."

My father shook his head. "They were seen. And the Prince's rooms in the palace are empty. It is no rumor."

I asked: "Edmund, too?"

"Yes," my father said. "But it is no disgrace to him. He obeys his father in this, as is proper. But for Stephen to run like a scared child..."

"He may find the going easier than the coming back," Peter said.

"That is what I want to talk to you about. As Peter knows and you too may have heard, Luke, there have been grumblings before about this Prince of ours, who has kept us five summers behind walls. If the Captains could have agreed on a successor he would have been deposed a year ago. This has brought them to the sparking point. They are agreed—all but his near kin and even some of those—that an end must be made."

Peter said doubtfully: "How? We have sworn loyalty to him, all of us. We asked the Spirits to take vengeance on us if we break our vows."

"Who crowned him?"

"Ezzard."

My father nodded. "In the name of the Spirits. And our oaths were made to him whom the Spirits, through Ezzard, named as Prince. What can be named can be unnamed."

"Has Ezzard done that?"

"The Captains have spoken to him and he has called a Seance for tomorrow noon."

"And will the Spirits unname him then?"

"You know Ezzard. He makes no promises. Nor can he. But the Spirits guard the city. Providing there is someone to take his place, I do not think Stephen will rule tomorrow night."

"Who have given way," Peter asked, "the Blaines or the Hardings?"

They were both great families, the Hardings with the longer lineage but the Blaines with, in recent years, more wealth and power. When my father had spoken about the difficulty of the Captains in agreeing on a successor to the Prince we had, I had guessed he was referring to the rival claims of these two factions.

My father said: "Neither as yet."

"But if they don't . . ."

"Neither will accept the other in authority over him. But they talk of the possibility of both accepting a third choice."

"Who is that?"

My father did not answer right away. I thought from his silence that it must be someone of whom he disapproved. He said slowly:

"This is why I called you to talk with me. There are risks, a dozen ways in which it could lead to disaster; and the disaster would fall on a man's sons as well as on himself."

I understood then. I did not say anything. I could not mistake my father's meaning but it was still incredible. He had been known as a great warrior in the time when the city's army went out to fight its enemies and I knew he was well liked among the Captains. But he had been born common, ennobled within the lifetime of his elder son.

They could not think of making him Prince in place of Stephen.

Peter said: "The honor is well deserved, sir. But . . ."

My father said: "I have put the questions to myself. Shall I tell you the answers I found in my mind?"

We waited for him to go on. He did not hurry. He was a man who thought slowly, except when he had a sword in his hand, and watched his words. He said:

"I found two answers. The first is that if the Blaines will not see the Hardings set above them, and the Hardings will not accept the Blaines, neither would wish to bow a knee to such as the Greenes or the Farrars." These were both important families in the city. "They would rather have a Prince whose father's adz marks can still be seen on the beams of their houses, which he helped build as a carpenter. It stings less."

I was not sure I agreed but I held my tongue. I thought of Henry and Gregory whom I had beaten in the Contest along with Edmund. With them, I felt, it would sting more, not less, if my father became Prince.

"The other answer stems from the first. A Prince of poor lineage will be a Prince, they may think, whom they can rule. He has the title but the Blaines and the Hardings will have the power. Until such a time as one or the other feels strong enough to act. And then such a Prince is someone that can be discarded, having fulfilled his purpose."

"The Spirits . . ."

"If the Spirits unmake one Prince they can unmake another. I do them honor, but Seers have acted under duress before, and the earth did not open up. I do not know that Ezzard would have called the Seance for tomorrow without a little prodding."

Peter said: "You can refuse, if you wish. No one can say it is from lack of courage. You could think it too high an honor."

"Do you say I should refuse?" my father asked him.

Peter said: "There are arguments on both sides. We accept your decision whatever it may be."

"And I will make it on my own judgment. But tell me what you think."

"You have said it: they plan to use you. It might be wiser to say no."

My father turned to me. "Luke?"

"Take it, sir!"

"You speak fiercely."

"He is very young." Peter smiled at me, though it was with affection. "And after winning his jeweled sword he lusts for action."

"Yes," my father said. "A good fault, but a fault. Your advice is better, Peter. You are beginning to acquire wisdom. All the same, I shall do as Luke urges. I am to be a weapon against the Prince, discarded when the crisis is past. But they may not find it so easy. I knew a Captain once, many years ago in the fighting against Alton, who was proud of a sword that was longer and sharper, he claimed, than any man's in the army. It slid off another's shield and hit his foot. It did not take it off, quite, but the surgeon did later. Weapons can turn in the hand.

"And there is another thing. Our forefathers were only common men but they lived in this city and fought for it. The Captains are right to turn against this Prince. The die has been cast and there must be bloodshed. For the city's welfare, for the common good, we must have a swift end to the struggle, not a long-drawn brawl that leaves us weakened."

Peter said: "We follow you, sir."

He bent his knee in the ceremonial bow that is made by a subject to his Prince. My father stared at him for a moment and then, smiling, clapped a hand on his shoulder.

"I am well defended! I had already decided what to say to Ezzard, but I shall do it with a lighter heart for that."

"To Ezzard? Not to the Captains?"

"To Ezzard first." He laughed. "We must give the Spirits time enough to prepare."

I met Martin next morning by the Ruins. There were other ruined buildings in the city, where people had not thought it worthwhile to clear the ground and build again, but these were by far the greatest and, it could be seen, of one vast building. Once, out of curiosity, I had measured the length of the mound of stone and it was more than two hundred paces. It staggered the mind to think of what it must have been like before the Disaster. Of course our Ancestors, as we knew, had used powers of magic for which the Spirits at last had punished them: how else could so monstrous a thing have been erected? They had buried their dead in its shade—there were worn stones bearing names and dates set in the ground—and it was said the Christians had used it as a place of worship. That, too, was hard to believe when one thought of the Christians in the city, a handful of wretches living mostly in the hovels by the North Gate, so warped and degraded that they accepted polymufs as members of their sect and as equals. (They would have accepted dwarfs, too, but got no chance: dwarfs had their pride.)

Although no one now would be so foolish as to build in stone it was used in foundations, and from time to time men took loads from the Ruins for this purpose. In doing so paths had been made in toward the center, and one led to a place where there was a hole in the ground and stairs leading to a vast cavernous place underneath. Boys would occasionally dare one another to venture down and the dares were taken; but no one went far in or stayed long.

Nor would I have done so, on my own, but Martin wanted to and I was determined not to show fear in front of him. We had explored it together, finding strange things—figures of men and women, carved life-size in stone, mildewed robes and banners, a pile of small pieces of colored glass. We also found a door, almost hidden by a heap of collapsed masonry, leading to a small room, and on Martin's urging we made a den there, furnishing it with a couple of wooden chairs we found in the outer part and taking in a stock of candles to give us light. It was cool in summer, warm in winter. We had sat and gossiped there through many a blank, wet day, private and secure from interruption. Martin, I knew, went down on his own as well, but I did not. And this morning I demurred at going down at all. It was not actually raining though the sky was a threatening gray. We stood and threw small stones at marks among the rubble. I was on edge, thinking of the Seance at noon and what might happen. I had not said anything to Martin, but he himself spoke of it.

I said, astonished: "How do you know that? It is supposed to be secret to the Captains."

He smiled. "The news is running through the city like wildfire. That the Prince is to be deposed and your father made Prince in his place."

Awkwardly, I said: "I'm sorry. I could not say anything. I was sworn to secrecy."

He nodded. "I thought so."

In his place, I knew, I would have been jealous and resentful because in the past we had kept no secrets from each other. But his mind was easier than mine, less given to brooding. I said:

"It may not happen like that, my father becoming Prince. So far it is only something suggested."

"It will happen. Everyone is sure of it. I suppose I shall see less of you from now on."

"I don't see why."

"As son of the Prince."

"What difference does that make?"

"And the Prince in Waiting."

This was the title given to the Prince's heir, who normally would expect to be Prince after him. Edmund had not had it but his elder brother, Charles. I said:

"But even if my father is Prince, that will be Peter, not I."

"Your mother will be Prince's Lady, not his."

"It is nothing to do with mothers. Peter is my father's eldest son, therefore he will be Prince in Waiting. He must be."

Martin shrugged. "That is not what people say. They say it was an omen, your winning the jeweled sword in the Contest."

"Then they say nonsense!"

I spoke angrily but I was not sure what it was that made me angry. My mind was confused. A magpie flew down into the Ruins and I threw a stone at it but missed by yards. I turned away and walked toward the High Street. Martin followed me. We walked together but in silence.

It was always dark inside the Seance Hall, there being only a few small windows to give light from outside, but since the Spirits did not manifest themselves by day the curtains had not been drawn and one could see without the aid of lamps. Only the first few rows were occupied, since the summoning had been merely of Captains and their sons. Ezzard stood in front of us and above us, on the platform that was carpeted in black, surrounded on three sides by and canopied in black velvet. He wore his Seer's robe of black silk, trimmed with white at cuffs and neck, and his white face stared down at us, sharp and deathlike.

He said: "The Spirits be with you."

We muttered back: "And with you, Seer."

"The Captains of this city," Ezzard said, "have called for guidance to the Spirits, as their forefathers did before them, begging the Spirits to help and advise them in a time of need, in the distress of the city. As Seer I have consulted with the Spirits and they have made answer: he who was Prince . . ."

There was a noise in the doorway. Ezzard halted his speech. We all looked and saw Prince Stephen standing there, Charles and Edmund behind him. After a pause, Ezzard went on:

"He who was Prince shall be Prince no longer. Forsaking the city in fear he loses right to the city's fealty . . ."

Prince Stephen interrupted him. He shouted:

"Ezzard, I left the city on your advice!" Ezzard watched him in silence. "On the warning of the Spirits, given through you."

"No."

"By the Great, it is true!" I heard his voice crack. "You told me . . ."

"I told you that the Spirits saw danger, to you and to your house. Anything more came from your own fears. And the Spirits spoke truly through me: the danger is here and now but your peril is of your own making, not due to the shivering of the earth."

"You let me think..."

"The Seer counsels the Prince; he is not required to teach him self-control. Even if the danger had been of earthquakes, would not a true Prince have looked after his people instead of fleeing from the city in panic?"

It was a charge that could not be answered. Prince Stephen tried, floundering:

"You said the Captains would see to it . . ."

"And they have." Ezzard looked away from him, to the Captains. "He who was Prince shall be Prince no longer. In his place the Spirits offer Captain Robert Perry for the approval of his peers. Does any man say no?"

There was silence. Ezzard said:

"Who acclaims?"

We all shouted together, in a roar which echoed. Ezzard said:

"Therefore, as Seer..."

Prince Stephen broke in again:

"I am Prince and this is treachery. I challenge the traitor to prove himself with his sword."

My father had no need to respond. He had been acclaimed by the Captains and so was Prince already. But we watched as he rose to his feet. He said:

"Not here, in the House of Spirits. We will see to this outside."

Ezzard said: "You are a dead man, Stephen. No man can fight when the Spirits forsake him."

There was an open yard between the Seance Hall and

Ezzard's house, which stood behind it, with a high fence on either side. We watched them fight there. By the standards that judges use in tournaments Stephen was a better swordsman than my father, who had learned his skill in battle, not from a fencing master. But under any circumstances my father's strength was much the greater. His sword smashed aside the thrusts and parries of the other, carelessly it seemed. And as Ezzard had said, what man could fight when the Spirits had forsaken him? Stephen's last throw had been hopeless when he made it, a desperate alternative to the miserable wandering exile which otherwise was the best future he could expect. He retreated a few times round the ring and then rushed on my father, offering no guard. My father's sword took him just beneath the ribs. He gasped and fell forward on it and blood gushed from his lips.

I was in my aunt's house the next day when my father came, his first visit to her since he had been made Prince. She called him Sire and bent her knee, but he shook his head, laughing.

"Leave that to the courtiers, Mary! It suits them better. I come here for peace and quiet."

She ordered Gerda to fetch ale and herself knelt and undid his boots. He said, looking round the small room, smoky from a fire that would not draw on a day of blustering wind:

"But we must find you a better place than this."

"It is good enough for me, Bob," she told him.

"But things have changed. You must learn to live like a Lady."

She said: "No, I am no Lady."

"That is soon remedied. The Prince makes whom he will noble."

"Not I."

"I say yes!"

"Please. Let me stay here as I am."

He looked at her. "Is there nothing you want?"

She put slippers on his feet. "For myself, nothing. I have it all."

That night Ezzard presided over a true Seance. We sat in darkness while the Spirits manifested themselves in strange sounds and sights: weird music, fluting high up in the rafters, tinkling bells, lights that moved across the blackness overhead, faces suddenly appearing as the Spirits put on again the flesh they had long outgrown. Voices.

A woman asked for help, her husband being sick, and was answered by the Spirit of her mother, ten years dead. She was told of herbs to pick, at a certain time and place, and of a broth to be made of them which would cure the sickness. There was a little dim light now, from the lamps of the Acolytes who stood on either side of the Hall, and I could see her, a small thin woman, nodding her understanding and thanks.

Others followed with questions. One of them, a farmer, said:

"I lost six lambs last year. I paid gold to the Seer for an audience and was told all would be well. This year I have lost eight. What of the promise?"

He spoke almost truculently. The Spirit who answered was that of his grandfather's father. He said:

"Thomas, you farm the land I farmed. Do you do your duty?"

"I do."

"Do you keep the laws?"

"I keep the laws."

"Then you would have prospered. Unless . . ."

"Unless what?"

"Unless you have kept Polybeasts that should have been killed at birth, and raised them for meat." There was a pause, but the farmer made no reply. "You lied, Thomas, when you said you kept the laws. That is why your flocks have sickened a second time. No gold will save him who defies the Spirits."

He went out, shuffling. There were others, some rebuked, some advised, some comforted. Then when the questions were over the little lamps were turned down again and the darkness returned. And in front of us a face grew, like a stern majestic man's but larger. A voice cried, deep and resonant:

"I speak, Stephen, Prince of this city in years gone by, ancestor of one who dishonored my name and lately died for it. The Spirits who guard this city have given you a new Prince. He will rule you well and lead your warriors to battle against your enemies—to battle and to victory."

There was a deep hush, not even a chair squeaking. The voice said:

"The Spirits crown your Prince."

It floated down from above, gently, gently, in the shape of a crown but having no substance, a faintly glowing crown of light. It came down to where my father sat, and hovered just above his head.

This, though a wonder, was expected. What followed was not. The voice spoke again:

"A great Prince and the father of one yet greater. His son shall be Prince of Princes!"

A second crown appeared out of the darkness. Peter stood on my father's right hand and I watched for it to move toward him, to rest over his head as the first one rested over my father's. And then my heart pounded, the blood dinned in my ears and I put my hand to the chair behind me so that I should not fall from dizziness. And my eyes were dazzled with the light shining down onto my upturned face.

four

The Prince
of Winchester

The summer of that year—a year that ended wretchedly—
was the happiest time of my life. This was not because the
Spirits had named me heir to my father, a future Prince of
the city. At least that did not seem to be the reason, though
I suppose it must have been a part of it. There was excitement in the air and the city buzzed with activity and
expectation. The resentments which had gathered over the
years against Prince Stephen's policy of skulking behind
walls turned into a feeling of release. It lifted my father
to a height of popularity which I do not think the other
Captains, when they acclaimed him, could have anticipa-
ted. Wherever he went in the city people crowded round
him, touching him when they could, blessing him in the
name of the Spirits. When he rode out at the head of his
army they cheered themselves silly: I saw a fat middle-aged

man, having been pushed or having stumbled to a fall, lying in the gutter but still yelling for the Prince. He was drunk, of course, from ale, but the whole city was drunk on the subtler brew of pride.

I had begged to be allowed to go with him on the campaign but had been refused. He smiled at me.

"In a couple of years you will have all the fighting you want. But even with a jeweled sword you are no match yet for the men of Alton. And though the Spirits having promised you a crown greater than your father's no doubt will protect you, they require a man to look to his own safety as well. The Spirits like to be respected but they are inclined to grow impatient with anyone who trusts to their help beyond common sense. This year you stay in the city."

Peter said: "There's a price to pay for everything, Luke, including being heir to the Princedom."

They smiled at each other and grinned at me. I had been uneasy with Peter after the Seance of the Crowns, thinking he must resent my being preferred over him, even though the preference was that of the Spirits. Even when he had congratulated me I had been wary, looking for signs hidden in his face and bearing. But I came to realize that there was nothing to find. His feelings for me were as warm and friendly as they had always been: he rejoiced in our father's rise to power and also in my being chosen heir.

We were in the palace. The room was quite small, merely an antechamber to the great Room of Mirrors which Stephen had most used for retirement. My father said it was too big: he did not like to hear his own voice echoing back at him. Nor did he care to see his own face whichever way he looked. So he had furnished the antechamber with simple things, including his wooden armchair from our old house, and he escaped there when court life bored him beyond bearing—which was not infrequently.

He said now to Peter: "A price for everything, you are right, and a duty, but the duties lie heavier on some than on others. I have never been a nay-sayer and I have already ordered the dwarfs to brew an ale to celebrate a victory at the Autumn Fair, but accidents can happen. I may fall off my horse and be trampled."

We smiled at that. He was a superb horseman, his horse, a big chestnut called Guinea, the surest-footed in the city's stables. He smiled as well, but went on:

"Or die of eating Alton's ailing cattle. If any such thing should happen, Peter, I leave you a duty, to look after Luke."

"I can look after myself," I said.

"I don't doubt it, but a wise man takes help where he can. As you know, there are some among those who have acclaimed me who do not wish me well. It did not please them when the Spirits crowned Luke. They are quiet just now because they have no choice. But if I were killed in battle . . ."

Peter nodded. "I follow that."

I said: "Watch whom you ride with, Father. The men of Alton may not be the only danger."

"Good advice, but I am already watching. That is part of being a Prince: one's eyes do not get much rest. And the more so in a case like mine, a man born common and chosen Prince because others with better claims could not resolve their quarrel." He looked at Peter. "You will see to this?"

"I will see to it," Peter said.

The person who was bitterly aggrieved by what had happened at the Seance, and showed it, was my Aunt Mary. When I went to her house, although she did not say anything and I sat down to dinner at her table as I had always done, I could tell her disapproval. It was not that she was sharper with me or smiled on me less—her tongue had always had a roughish edge and her face did not seem to have been made for smiling—but I sensed resentment, anger, in small looks she gave me. I was not surprised by this. Peter meant everything to her, and had since my father divorced her. Peter was my father's eldest son, born in wedlock, and his natural heir. What the Spirits said meant nothing to her; she would have defied all the Spirits in the universe for Peter's sake.

I thought that her disappointment and bitterness would lessen with time and for a week or two carried on with my visits as though nothing had happened. Then one day I went to her house following heavy rain. I cleaned my muddy boots on the scraper outside her door but did not do it well enough, and there were dirty footprints on the polished boards of her little hall.

She saw them and tongue-lashed me. It was a thing she

had done before, but again I found a difference in the scolding, a note of hatred almost. And she said:

"Even if you are to be Prince of Princes, you can still wipe your boots before you enter this house. Or do you already think we should all be servants, to do your bidding?"

The jibe stung and I felt myself flushing. She finished:

"Take your boots off, wash your hands, and come to the table."

Gerda the polymuf had heard her, and I was the Prince's son and heir. I looked at her, my own anger sharp:

"No, thank you. I will eat at the palace."

And I turned, saying no more, and left her house. I have wondered since whether things might not have fallen out differently if I had contained my rage, accepted the rebuke, and eaten my dinner with her that day. Or if I had done as I intended next morning and gone to make amends. But I thought that when I went she would scold me further and my pride would not bear it. Two days later I saw her in the street. We approached from opposite directions, saw each other but did not show it, and I was torn between the desire to go to her and the fear that she would treat my overture with scorn. We were near the Buttercross and there were boys I knew sitting on the steps there: they would see and probably hear all that happened. So I passed her in silence with the smallest of nods to which she made no acknowledgment.

After that it was, of course, even more difficult to put

things right, and with the passage of time, impossible. I missed her, but there were so many things to do that I forgot about her most of the time. For her, though, there were no such distractions. She had never had much to do with her neighbors. When I stopped going to her house—and a little later my father and Peter rode away on the campaign against Alton—she must have been lonely there with no company except the two polymuf maids and her cat. I did not think of that then, though I did later.

If my father's triumph had turned sour for Aunt Mary, my mother reveled in the change. She had always been a sunny person but was happier than ever in being the Prince's Lady. She had new dresses made, a dozen at least, in bright silks and satins and brocades, and a polymuf woman whose entire concern was to arrange her hair each day. There were no housewifely duties anymore—a butler saw to everything—and all she need do was look beautiful. She had always had beauty, but as a precious stone is made ten times more splendid by its setting, so hers was enhanced by the things my father lavished on her. She adorned herself to delight him, and he showed his joy in her. He said once when she told him (not seriously, I fancy) that he spent too much on her that it was for this reason only that he had become Prince.

Although there were things to do in which he could not accompany me I still spent a lot of time with Martin. With him I could forget about being the son of the Prince and there were times when, however much I enjoyed my new life, I was glad of this. We rode together—I found a pony for him in the palace stables—and fished for trout and explored the country for miles beyond the city boundaries. Once, deep in a wood, we found a dozen cherry trees laden with fruit. The fruits were so big and juicy, for all the long neglect of the trees, that we thought they might be polymuf cherries, but we ate them no less heartily for that and with no worse result than an ordinary griping that evening from having gorged ourselves.

We had one falling out. It happened in our den under the Ruins. We had arranged to meet there and I was late. I found him reading a book by candlelight. He looked up and greeted me. I asked him:

"What's that you've got?"

Books were rare things—few of the common people could read and not all the nobles—and this one looked strange. Its covers were not stiff but limp, and the shape was odd: higher and wider than usual, but thin. There had been a picture on the front which damp had turned into a meaningless mess of colors, but I could read words across the top: POPULAR MECHANIX. "Popular" I knew, but "Mechanix" meant nothing to me.

Martin said: "I was digging in the rubble at the back of Clegg's." That was the baker's shop in the High Street. "I saw the corner of an old cupboard—I suppose the quake moved whatever was on top of it—and I thought I'd see if there was anything inside. There were only books. Most of them were rotten but this one wasn't too bad.

There was a strangeness in his manner—part excitement, part something else. I went round behind him to have a look. There was a picture on the page where he had the book open. Because it had faded I could not tell what it was at first. Then I saw and knew what the something else was. It was guilt. The book was a relic from olden days: the picture was a picture of a machine.

I could not tell what kind of machine it was and did not want to. I put my hand over his shoulder, sweeping the book from his grasp. It fell closed on the floor and I put my foot on it.

He said, sharply for Martin: "Don't do that!"

"A forbidden thing..."

"I was only looking at it."

"That makes no difference. You know it doesn't. Seeing is thinking and thinking is as bad as doing. Have you forgotten old Palmer?"

He had lived in a cottage outside the city walls, a long way from the road. A peddler, desperate to sell his goods, had called there one day and later reported what he had seen: this man, neither farrier nor armorer nor metalworker, was brazing metal and building something from it. The soldiers rode out of the Prince's command and took him. He was tried and found guilty and hanged. For a week his body hung on the gibbet outside the North Gate.

Martin said: "He was *making* a machine. And in his cottage, where anyone might find out. We are the only ones who know this place. I have not shown the book to anyone else and will not. I will hide it; not even in here. Under rubble, outside."

"But it is a forbidden thing! Whether you are discovered or not, that is true."

"But why forbidden?"

"You do not need to ask that. Because our ancestors made machines and the machines destroyed the earth, causing earthquakes and volcanoes that killed men by the hundreds of thousands. That is why the Spirits decreed that the making of machines was an abomination."

"I suppose there were bad machines. But there may have been others as well. This one—I cannot follow the details properly—but it is about something that cuts grass. How could that cause earthquakes and volcanoes?"

"I tell you the Spirits condemn machines. All machines."

"The Spirits, or the Seers?"

"The Seers are the servants of the Spirits."

"Or their masters."

"You must be mad! No man can rule the Spirits, who are eternal."

"If they exist."

"You have seen and heard them."

"I have seen strange things, in the dark."

"That is blasphemy!"

I spoke in anger. I almost hit him, moving a step forward and doubling my fist. We stared at each other in the flickering candle's light; then I stooped and picked up the book. Martin made no protest as I shredded the pages: they were not parchment but made of some flimsier material. There were more pictures of machines and I averted my eyes so as not to see them. He watched me as I crumpled the pages on the floor and put the candle flame to a corner of one. They burned slowly because there was no draft down here, and smokily. When the heap was charred and black I put my heel on it and ground it into fine ash.

I said: "I'm going up now. There might be news of the fighting. Are you coming?"

He nodded. "All right."

I wanted to tell him why I had been angry. Not because of the blasphemy in itself but because of the risks that it involved. It was true that he had only said these things to me and in a place where we were quite alone, but even that was dangerous. What point was there in giving word to thoughts like that? One took risks, in battle for instance, but only for a worthwhile end. There was none here.

But I said nothing because, my anger cooling, I thought it best to let it all drop, to forget this unprofitable and perilous subject. We did not talk about it again except one night, weeks later, when we stood together on the northern wall and watched the red glow of the Burning Lands beyond the hills. As we looked a spot brightened, sign of a new eruption. Martin said:

"How could they have caused it?"

"What?"

"The machines. How could any machine make the earth produce burning mountains? I have listened to a man who has seen them quite close. Thousands of feet high, he said. How could any machine do that?"

I said: "It doesn't matter how. And it is not worth talking about. It happened, and that's enough."

I was not angry now but anxious for him. For myself, too. I could hear voices from an alehouse behind and beneath us, spilling out through the night air. But Martin said no more.

I had the chance of making many new friends at that time. Boys, of my own age and older, paid me a lot of attention, seeking my company and flattering me when they had it. I suppose something of the sort might have happened simply because of my victory in the Contest, but of course there was more to it than that. From being nobody, the second son of an obscure Captain, I had become the Prince's heir.

This flattery did not please me as at one time I would have thought it would. On the contrary the few fits of depression I endured during that splendid summer were directly caused by it; because it all seemed meaningless when it was lavished on me and worse than meaningless: destructive. The victory had been a true one, and hard-earned; my father's acclamation and the honor paid me by the Spirits were both great things. To hear them mouthed by sycophants was to have them cheapened, and I was forced to turn away before they were made entirely worthless. Two or three times I went back to my room in the palace, not wanting even to see Martin, and lay on my bed, my thoughts black with despair. What sense was there in striving for anything, when all achievement ended as the prey of mean minds? But the moods were few, and they passed quickly.

I knew what was said of me when I turned away—that my head had been swollen by my success and my father's, that I was too proud to mix with those I deemed lesser mortals. So at times I gritted my teeth and made an effort to put up with them; not because I cared much for their opinions but because these were my father's subjects and would, in due course, be mine. Between a Prince and his people there must be good will or at least its semblance. I do not know how far I succeeded in my wooing of them. Not much, I fancy. My heart was never in it.

The one whom I did take to my heart and who became my second friend, strangely enough, was Edmund. My father had been magnanimous in his dealings with Stephen's family. There had been some who had argued that his sons should be killed and many who had favored exiling them from the city. They had stood with their father in defying the Spirits and removing them meant removing a future danger. But my father would have none of this. They had done their duty as sons in supporting their father and provided they made due allegiance to the new Prince no harm should come to them: Charles was permitted to keep his Captaincy.

But their position was a poor one. Poor as far as money was concerned—their father's goods were forfeit and they and their mother went to live in a small house, a hovel almost, in Salt Street—and poor in reputation. No one now had a good word to say for the dead Prince and his sons incurred the same scorn. The boys who crowded round me spurned Edmund, whom a few weeks earlier they had courted.

One day I was with a group of boys at the Buttercross when Edmund joined us. There had already been attempts to make an Ishmael of him by showing that he was unwelcome, but he had stubbornly refused to accept it. The boys started this again and one of them said something about a smell of death and traitors. Others laughed. I saw Edmund go white. He said:

"My father was no traitor, but killed by one. A traitor from a gutter in Dog Alley . . . and now you lick his boots!"

It was true that my father had been born in that street, one of the meanest in the city. The eyes of the others watched me greedily to see what I would do. I did not want to fight him here, in front of them. I made a jest instead.

"Dog Alley—that runs into Salt Street, doesn't it?"

They laughed in support of me. Edmund said:

"Yes. Times change. Scum comes to the top."

He spat at my boots as he said that. I had no choice but to hit him. They formed a ring around us, and we fought.

His family had been noble as long as could be remembered in the city—since the Disaster, it was said—and he had a look of breeding, being tall with a long face, thin lips, arrogant blue eyes. But he was strong, too, and he fought with the anger pent up since his father's death. He threw me and leaped on me. I rolled clear and got to my feet. We grappled and he threw me again. He knelt on me trying to spread-eagle my arms. Panting, sobbing almost, he whispered: "Scum ... scum!"

I realized I could be beaten, disgraced before this mob, and the demon inside me rose in a fury to match his. I tore free and as he came for me got a wrist and brought him across my body to land heavily on the cobbles. The blow winded him but he was up as soon as I was. He came at me. I straight-armed him, punching to the body. He winced and tried to hide it.

After that I kept him at a distance. Although he was the taller my arms were longer. My demon served me well as he always did. There are some who fight wildly in the rage of battle, their minds hot and confused, but mine goes cold and thoughts come quicker and more sharply. I concentrated on body blows, on that vulnerable part between and just below the ribs. These sapped his strength. He went on fighting and once succeeded in throwing me a third time but he could not press it home. I was up before he was and punched him as he rose. From that point it was only a question of how long he would last. It seemed an age to me and I was giving the punishment, not receiving it. I had switched my attack to his face which was smeared with blood. At last he dropped and could not even attempt to rise.

Our audience was cheering me and mocking him. I went to the horse trough below the Buttercross, soaked my handkerchief, and returned to bathe his face. It was swelling already and would look terrible in a few hours.

I said: "It was a good fight. The Spirits were on my side."

He stared at me, making no answer. I crumpled the hand-kerchief in my pocket and put an arm out to him.

"You are filthy, and so am I. Let's leave this lot." I gave my head a small contemptuous jerk in the direction of the watching circle. "Come back with me, and we'll get ourselves cleaned up."

"Back" meant the palace, which had been his home. He still did not speak and I thought he would refuse. But at last he nodded slightly. I helped him up and we went off together. The onlookers parted to give us way and watched us go in puzzled silence.

After that Edmund and I were friends. One day the three of us—he and Martin and I—were strolling down the High Street past the Seance Hall when the Seer came out. He stopped and spoke, addressing himself to me.

"You keep strange company, Luke."

I said: "It is the company I choose, sire, and which chooses me."

The remark must have been aimed at Edmund—he had seen Martin and me together often enough—and I did not like it. It was said that the Seer had been among those who were for killing the sons of Stephen, and I supposed he was angry that Edmund had escaped and angrier that I should befriend him. But he went on:

"It is good to see quarrels mended before they become feuds." He turned to Edmund. "Your brother is with the Army?"

"Yes, sire."

There was something in his voice which was not quite contempt but a long way from the deference which was reckoned to be the Seer's due. He had not been to a Seance, I knew, since his father's death. He believed in the Spirits, I think, and acknowledged their power, but hated them. His long face was without expression but I saw scorn in the blue eyes under the high forehead.

Ezzard, disregarding this, if indeed he saw it, said:

"He fought well in the battle."

"What battle?" I asked.

"The battle at Bighton, where Alton was defeated."

I stared at him. "We have only just come from the Citadel. There is no news yet. The pigeons have brought none."

Ezzard smiled his thin cold smile. "The Spirits do not have to wait on the wings of pigeons."

"This is from the Spirits?"

"Would I tell you else?"

"And a victory?" Martin asked. "At Bighton?"

"The pigeons are already flying," Ezzard said. "They will be in their cotes before sunset."

It must be true. I asked:

"And my father . . .?"

"The Prince is safe."

I was too excited to speak further. But Martin said:

"How do they bring the news?" Ezzard looked at him. "The Spirits? If not on wings, how?"

Ezzard said: "A wise man, or boy, does not ask questions concerning the Spirits. They tell him what he needs to know. That is enough."

It was a rebuke, but Martin persisted. "But you know things about the Spirits, sir, since you serve them and talk with them. Is that not true?"

"I know what I am told, boy."

"But more than the rest of us do? How they bring their messages without wings, perhaps?" Ezzard's eye was on him. "I am not asking how, sir—just if you do know."

"I know many things," Ezzard said, "and I keep my knowledge to myself, imparting it only to those who have dedicated their lives to serve the Spirits. Would you do that, Martin? Would you be an Acolyte?"

It was a good reply, and one that must stop his questioning. Even if I had not heard him blaspheming the idea would have been ridiculous. One would have to be crazed to be an Acolyte—shaving one's head, fasting, droning prayers to the Spirits all day and half the night. I expected him to be abashed.

But to my astonishment he said: "I might, sir."

Ezzard stared at him keenly, nodded, and went his way. Edmund and I poked fun at Martin when he had gone. He joined with us. It had been a joke, he said, at the Seer's expense; and the old fool had believed him! I accepted what he said but I was still not sure. I had watched his eyes as well as the Seer's. If the earnestness had been deception it had been marvelously done.

Two days later I stood on the walls by the North Gate and heard the wild cheers of the crowd as our army returned victorious. A big man led them on a big chesnut horse: my father, Prince of Winchester.

five

FIRE IN WINTER

The victory over Alton was overwhelming. Five Captains were taken for ransom, including the Prince's nephew—his probable heir since he had only one son whose poor health prevented his being a warrior. A sixth Captain had been killed and they left more than three score men dead or badly injured on the field. We for our part had one Captain crippled and scarcely more than twenty men dead or seriously wounded.

We had a triumphant Autumn Fair. They had ceded the village of Bighton to us, and altogether over a hundred thousand acres of land. Feasting went on for more than a week and the special ale my father had ordered the ale-makers to brew was exhausted in half that time, in toasts to his health and the city's victory. (There was no shortage of milder ale and they strengthened it with raw spirits;

men lay drunk in the streets not just at night but at broad noon.) The Hardings and the Blaines were quiet, raising their glasses with the rest but doubtless thinking their own thoughts. These were mixed, I fancy. I have no doubt they rejoiced in our triumph, for which they themselves had fought also, but it could not have pleased them to see so much honor paid to their stopgap Prince. We guessed that behind locked doors they were talking hard, with grim faces.

When the Fair was over and the prisoners exchanged for Alton gold, the Court rode out to hunt. I was one of the party, for the first time. I asked that Martin and Edmund might come also but my father would not agree: to belong to the royal hunting party was a great privilege which must not be awarded lightly. Martin was a commoner and it would be a scandal if Edmund, son of a man condemned by the Spirits, were included. Martin, I knew, was not sorry about this; he was neither fighter nor hunter by nature though he had helped me in the Contest. I had seen him turn pale when we watched a pig's throat being slit at the slaughterhouse. But for Edmund, though he said nothing, it was salt rubbed into unhealed wounds. This would have been his first year for the hunt also.

One of the things that had made the summer memorable had been the weather. It was not just that it seemed better to me (one sees brighter skies in times of happiness): others, even the old ones, agreed that it was many years since we had been so fortunate. For more than a month, in July and August, no fires were lit in the palace except those in the kitchens. Very often the sun shone clearly, sometimes through the whole day with cloud obscuring it for no more than an hour or two. The harvest was good: all the granaries were filled and corn piled in bins in the mills.

And the sun which had shone on my rambles with Martin and Edmund and on my father's campaign had not yet deserted us. We rode to the hunt on a morning sharp but clear; frost crackling in the grass under our horses' hoofs, but the sky blue all round. I read a book once, the ink in places fading from the parchment, in which it was said that before the Disaster the sun shone almost all the time in summer. I had thought it a fantasy like some of the other things written there—as, for instance, that one of the wonders with which the devils seduced our ancestors before they destroyed them was the power to talk with and even see one another when they were a hundred miles or more apart. But now I could almost believe it. I was sorry for Edmund, left behind in the city, but it was impossible not to take joy in the air's crisp freshness, the horse under me, all the colored beauty of the dying year.

We rode south, following the river, toward the forest of Botley. There had always been boar there and it had long been a royal hunt, but new stories had come back lately from the country people who lived on the outskirts of the forest. Their fields had been attacked by beasts of incredible size and wiliness. Polymufs, they said, and implored the Prince to destroy them.

It was forbidden to keep polymuf cattle or poultry: all

deformed creatures must be destroyed and burned or buried. (There were some who would have done the same with polymuf children, but the Spirits decreed that they should live, though separate from proper men and serving them.) Wild polybeasts were killed also, within civilized lands. Elsewhere, in the barbarous places, it was said they lived and flourished, in all sorts of strange and monstrous forms, from rats that built houses, or at least mounds to dwell in, to the terrible Bayemot that destroyed everything in its path. From time to time, polybeasts came down into our lands and when they did it was the Prince's duty to exterminate them. Not that we believed these boar were polymuf: country people are given to exaggeration and alarm. But a boar hunt was justification in itself.

We found nothing on the first day. We came on their spoor—tracks and droppings—but they were not, in the judgment of Bannock, the Master of the Hunt and one with great skill in reading signs, even fresh. Tents were set up that night in the fields by Shidfield village. My father had been offered lodging but declined, on the grounds of not inconveniencing the villagers; but as he said, laughing in private, also because he had never yet encountered a village lodging that was not overrun with fleas, and polymuf giant fleas at that. As it was, they brought meat and ale to us, and bread and cheese and honey cakes. Of no high quality: if it was their best, my father said, they deserved to have their taxes remitted on grounds of poverty, but he had no doubt it was not their best. They too were aware of conclusions that might be drawn and were wary. After being entertained by them three years before, Prince Stephen had increased their tax assessment.

On the second day we drew boar and killed two. They were good specimens but although Bannock examined them long and carefully he found no trace of polymuf. We roasted one that night on a spit turned by two kitchen lads recruited from the village. The flesh was good and sweet. We killed another beast on the morning of the third day, an old tusker who crippled two dogs before Captain Nicoll ran him through. On the fourth day we found the polymuf.

We had ranged farther from our base, to a new part of the forest. The trees for the most part were thin enough for us to ride without difficulty, but there were patches of thicker growth. Spoor was found which impressed Bannock: the hoof marks were very big indeed, and the droppings also. We cast around and the dogs at last gave tongue. They led us to a stretch of dense undergrowth. While the beaters were working round it the beast broke cover and rushed straight for our lines.

It was enormous, five feet from ground to shoulder and large in proportion. And it moved fast, more like a horse than a boar. It got through while two men stabbed futilely at it with their spears. We turned to give chase but as my horse's head came round I saw with astonishment that the beast had also turned, with amazing agility, and was heading back toward us. I did not waste time thinking about this but, realizing that it was coming my way, set my lance and spurred my horse to meet it.

All I saw was a massive blur of motion, gray and hairy, racing through the trees. Perhaps my horse saw more, or more clearly. At any rate he reared in fright. In controlling him I let my lance tip hit the ground. With bucking horse and the shock from the lance I could not keep my seat. I hit the ground, rolling to break my fall. I was cursing my misfortune and the fact that there was now another gap for the boar to break through our lines a second time. I looked for it and saw it. It was not going for the gap. It had changed its course and was bearing down on me. I could see it well enough now, see red-rimmed eyes and the savage white gleam of tusks. I tried to get to my feet and realized, as pain shot down my leg, that I was injured. Voices shouted, but a long way off. The boar smashed a bush aside like straw. The sight of it, almost on me, and its stink dried my throat with fear. Then from my left there were hammering hoofs. I saw a horse and rider and a lance which raked the boar along its ribs, forcing it away with a huge squeal of pain. The horse cleared me as I lay there. The rider was Peter, who had stayed close by me throughout the hunt.

He had not killed the boar but the wound helped the rest to run it down within an hour and dispatch it. It was a fearsome beast, I was told, seven feet in length from snout to tail. The size alone branded it polymuf but apart from that it was double-tusked and its head was bigger in relation to its body than was usual. A polymuf strain was sometimes thought to be an indication of greater intelligence, as with the building rats that tales were told of, and this one seemed to have behaved with more than mere cunning, in doubling back to attack its enemies and in going for me when it saw me unhorsed. I gather it led them a fine dance before they finished it off.

My father said he would have dearly liked its head to hang on the palace wall: Bannock, in more than thirty years of hunting, had never seen anything that could come near matching it for magnificence. But the law held. They built a pyre and left the carcass burning. I did not see anything of this, having been helped back to the camp after Bannock had set my leg, broken in the fall.

I was taken back on a litter strapped between quiet horses. For two more weeks I had to lie on my bed, my leg splinted. After that for long enough I hobbled with a crutch. My friends came to see me to help me pass the time, Martin every day but Edmund less frequently. I knew why: it was still an ordeal for him to come to the palace, and I guessed he had to steel himself afresh on each occasion.

Autumn closed into winter. The good weather had broken even before the hunt was over and we paid for past beneficence with freezing fogs and, in early October, with blizzards that sent snow whirling round the city walls, piling high against houses, blocking the streets and drifting up against the windows of the palace to obscure my view out over the town. In other years I had loved the coming of the first snow, when gangs of boys were formed in snow-ball fights that raged all day (apart from the break for dinner at midday) through the grazing meadows and even up into the streets of the town until our elders put a stop to it. I was past the age for that, and for skating: my enforced inaction only emphasized my inability to take part, but it emphasized my boredom, too. I played games with Martin —chess and checkers and liars' dice—but he beat me too easily at the first two and I won too easily at the third: he had no guile.

In November my father went to Romsey, to visit the Prince of that city. Prince Stephen's refusal to send his army into the field, his reliance on walls built higher every year, had been part of a more general isolation. There had been no state visits, made or received, for some time. My father's accession, followed by his victory over Alton, had changed that. It was not only Romsey that wished to see the new Prince of Winchester.

My father took his bodyguard with him, of course, and a few of his Captains, but for show rather than protection. Men did not make war in the winter and such a visit as this was in any case safeguarded under the customs of all civilized peoples. We waved him good-by as he and his entourage rode out from the South Gate and then we turned back to our ordinary occasions. Dull always at this time of the year—halfway between the Autumn Fair and the Christmas Feast—I found them duller still with my father away, and the summer's excitements fading into memory. The days passed and the evenings lengthened as winter tightened its grip. I wearied of games played by lamplight, and of the amusements which delighted my mother and her friends: the polymuf jugglers and clowns, the guitarists strumming and singing melancholy love songs. My leg was still splinted so I could not ride during the day. I was restless, bored, wanting something to happen. But when it did happen it was not during the dragging day or tedious evening but at night, while the palace slept.

I awoke to a smell that was so strong one almost tasted it, and sat up coughing, the smoke in my throat and lungs. It was pitch black. I hobbled to my window and flung the shutters open. Cold fresh air streamed in. The night was dark apart from the glow of the Burning Lands, and a light nearer at hand, blossoming from a window beneath me, and with it the dreaded crackling that told of fire.

I shouted an alarm and, wasting no more time, headed for the door and the stairs. My room was to the right of the staircase, my mother's apartments on the far side of it. But as I opened the door the crackling was more like a roar and automatically I shielded my face from the light and the heat. The staircase was a torrent of flame, spreading, moving upward. It had passed the landing and was ravenously eating its way up toward the attics.

If I could leap it, I thought, and get across to where she was . . . The surgeon had said my splints could come off in a few days. I got back to my room and, needing no light from the brilliance of the fire behind me, found my knife and slashed the binding cords. My leg was terribly weak and I winced with the pain of putting my weight on it, but it would do. I headed back to the staircase.

It was impossible. In the short time I had been away, a matter of seconds only, the fire had spread and strengthened. It was frightening to look at, like a living creature in its raging hunger and power. I could not get within feet of it without being scorched.

There was another chance. Wooden gutterings ran along the side of the building, below the windows. I got to my bedroom and clambered out, holding onto the sill with my hands. People were gathering in the courtyard, more than twenty feet below. I heard their voices, shouting, calling, a woman screaming, and tried to ignore them. The gutterings were wide and shallow and I had already discovered that one could use them to get from room to room. It was not easy—one had to stand on this narrow ledge and inch one's way along with one's face flat against the wall—but it was possible. I started on my way. I thought only of my progress, closing my mind to everything else: to what I would do if I reached her and also to the terrifying possibility of a misstep.

But what I could not close my mind to was the increasing heat of the boards against which I was pressed. The fire, triumphant inside, was beating out against its confines. In a spot where the timbers were not properly caulked I caught a glimpse of the furnace within. But I was getting past the worst, I thought, the part that lay over the staircase. I risked a look in the direction in which I was edging and saw no sign of flame. I had come at least a dozen feet and probably had no more than that to go before reaching a window. I was cool in mind and increasingly confident. And I remember no more until the point at which I woke up, in bed, in daylight, my head splitting with pain.

One of the pegs that supported the guttering, weakened by the heat perhaps, had given way and I had fallen. A soldier in the crowd below had tried to break my fall. He succeeded in part—my recently knitted leg did not snap again—but my head struck something which knocked me unconscious and, as sometimes happens, took away my recollection of the accident as well.

Wilson told me this, sitting beside my bed with his long face, never much better than melancholy, a solemn mask. He was Sergeant in charge of the palace, an old and well-trusted follower of my father. They had served in the ranks together as young men. My father, on becoming Prince, had wanted to make him a Captain, to ennoble him, but he would not have it. He had had a wife many years before but she had died, broken-hearted, after giving birth to a polymuf child. He had not married again and apart from my father had no real friends.

My mind was confused, my head aching. I sat up and it was worse. Wincing, I said:

"And the fire? What happened . . .?"

"That wing is gutted. The rest was saved."

I think it was his look of misery which recalled what my own purpose had been. I said:

"My mother . . ."

He shook his head very slowly. No more was needed. I could not believe it, though I knew it was true. I had seen her only a few hours before, her eyes half closed, foot tapping, head slightly swaying to a tune she loved. She was fond of music which I was not. I had slipped away without,

I now remembered so sharply, bidding her good night.

I concentrated my wits and asked Wilson questions, which he answered. I think he thought me strange, perhaps callous, to do so at such a time; but it seemed to me that my sorrow was my own, a private thing, and not to be talked over even with one so well known and well trusted as Wilson. Pigeons, he told me, had been sent to Romsey, calling my father back. To my query as to how the fire had started he said it was fairly sure it had been deliberate, a murderous act. This had always seemed likely because, living in wooden houses as we did, we observed strict precautions against accidental fire. A special patrol checked the palace each night. But it was not a matter of supposition only. One of the guard had found a polymuf watching the fire from hiding. He had flint and steel on him, and oil-soaked wadding. Moreover he was known for a crazy loon who loved playing with fire. There had been trouble before and he had been exiled in the end; he was not allowed in the city and lived in a ramshackle hut beneath St. Catharine's Hill, shunned even by the other polymufs.

I asked: "How did he get into the city?"

Wilson shrugged. "It is not difficult."

That was true. The gate guards were supposed to check all who passed through but I had myself slipped past their backs when I did not want to call attention to myself.

"And why the palace?"

Wilson said: "That will bear looking into."

"Has he been questioned?"

"No. We await your father's return. But we have him

safe. I set the guards myself. No one will get to him, either to rescue him or to close his mouth."

"No other trouble?"

If this were a plot, laid by the Hardings or the Blaines, maybe both, now would be the moment to rise, before my father could get back. I saw by Wilson's face that he took my meaning.

"No trouble. And we are ready for any that comes."

My father was back before evening. It snowed heavily in the afternoon, obliterating the familiar tracks, but that did not stop him. He rode up through the city streets and into the courtyard in advance of his laboring escort. I heard a distant cry—"The Prince!"—and the clatter of hoofs on stone and ran to the window of the room in which I had been bedded. I saw him dismount, a snow man from a snow horse, and stand there, staring in front of him, while the horse was taken by a groom.

He was looking at the wing in which we had lived. It was a sight I had already seen, with sickness and a sad thumping of the heart. The snow, which had mostly been cleared from the courtyard, lay thick there, in uneven mounds from which a few blackened upright timbers pointed toward the gray sky. It was a whiteness and desolation that chilled the blood, a wilderness made more horrifying by the buildings which still stood all round. I saw him take a step, as though to go toward it and then with a twist of his head turn away. Then I called to him from the window; in a low voice, but he heard me and looked up.

Even from that distance and with the light beginning to fade I could see the grief and anger in his face.

I threw clothes on and, ignoring the protests of the nurse who was attending to me, hurried downstairs. I found my father in the Great Hall along with others—Peter, three of his Captains, and a number of commoners, including Wilson. Wilson was talking, telling the story of what had happened, and my father was listening. His face was a cold hard mask now. He said at the end:

"Has the polymuf talked yet?"

"Only in crazed words."

"Have him brought in."

Peter said: "It may be he acted on his own. He is known to be a lunatic."

"Yes," my father said, "well known. And therefore a good weapon to another's hand."

Neither Blaine nor Harding was there, and none closely linked with them. If the polymuf had been set on by someone, I wondered which. Perhaps both. They had made no move but it might have been their plan not to—to wait until my father's return and attack then, while he was shattered by the earlier blow. He looked like a man of iron, waiting for the polymuf to be brought. If they thought a blow could shatter him they were in for a surprise.

The polymuf, his hands chained, was pushed forward by the guards and sprawled at my father's feet. I recognized him as one I had seen wandering alone in the fields beyond the East Gate. The Spirits had marked him with a hare lip, fissured red up to the nostril, and his voice showed that his mouth had no roof. He lay on the floor and talked nonsense, the words themselves scarcely understandable. I heard him babble about fire . . . the Spirits . . . death . . . and fire again.

My father stooped down and took him by the hair. He said:

"Who told you to do this?"

His voice was cold and sharp; only his eyes blazed with anger. The polymuf spoke again, but still in nonsense. My father shook him, with force enough to send his legs skittering across the polished boards but not letting go of his hair. The polymuf howled. My father said:

"I have a gift for you, polymuf. Tell me who put you up to it and you die quickly. It is a good reward. I do not think you care for pain." He shook him a second time, a dog with a rat. "There was another. Was there not?"

"Yes!" the polymuf cried. "Yes, Lord . . ."

"Name him."

"Not a man. It was . . ."

My father dragged him upright and stared into his face. "Do not say it was the Spirits or I will not keep my temper."

"Not the Spirits. It was . . ."

I thought I grasped the words but he spoke so badly I could not be sure. And it made no sense. My father said:

"Say again."

"Your Lady, Lord."

"You fool!" my father shouted. "Are you saying my

Lady told you to light the torch that burned her? You get no gift for that. You will . . ."

"Your other Lady, Lord!" My father's hand dropped from him as though it too was scorched with flame. "She who lives on the River Road."

At first my Aunt Mary denied everything, claiming that the story was an invention of the polymuf to save himself from torture. But when she was confronted by a farm worker, who had seen her coming away from the polymuf's hut, she fell silent. Thereafter during her trial she did not speak, not even when the sentence of death by burning was pronounced on her. I was in the court and saw her eyes go to my father's but I do not think it was in appeal. It was his gaze that, after a moment, turned away. Her look followed him while she was being taken off by the guards.

The execution was fixed for the next day. That evening I had word that she wished to see me. It was her polymuf servant, Gerda, who brought it. She had been weeping, it was plain, and wept again when I hesitated.

"Master Luke, I beg you! For a few minutes only."

I had never heard my aunt give her anything but scoldings but her grief might have been for a mother. That by itself would not have persuaded me to go. It was my aversion which did so. I had felt for my aunt, since I heard the accusation that spilled from the lips of the crouching polymuf in the Great Hall, both horror and a kind of fear. I would not give in to this. I told the maid I would see her.

The Sergeant of the prison guard demurred at first about admitting me. When he did, he accompanied me to the cell and himself stood there while we talked. From time to time he cast my aunt uneasy glances, as though fearing that, although unarmed and helpless, she could by some witch's art strike me dead.

She looked very old in the gray shapeless felon's gown. And feeble, though I knew she had not been put to torture. But her eyes were as sharp and strong as ever; and her mind had not budged from its single concern. She asked me:

"Where is Peter?"

"Under guard."

"What will they do with him?"

I hesitated. In fact, I did not know. There had been no evidence to link him with the crime but to some it was condemnation enough that it had been done for his sake. Others said that even if not treacherous in the past he could not be trusted now, the son of such a mother.

My aunt said: "Speak for him, Luke."

I said: "It was me you wanted dead, Aunt, wasn't it? Not my mother."

She shook her head, as though impatient, almost angry, at an irrelevance. She said:

"Peter knew nothing of it. You must believe that."

"You wanted me dead."

Her eyes met mine, unwavering. "Only because you were named heir. There was no right in it. My son is the elder, born in wedlock."

"The Spirits named me."

"There was no right in it," she repeated.

"You would do it again, if you could."

I did not say that as a question, although in my mind still it was a question. I could not believe that she had tried to kill me. She looked at me.

"Yes."

"And you ask me to speak for Peter?"

"They are burning me tomorrow. Is that not enough? And Peter saved your life in the hunt."

"To your regret."

"No. I would not have him different from what he is."

"But were ready to kill to make him heir."

Weariness for a moment showed through her determination. She said:

"What he is and what I would do for him are different things. I will pay for my part, in the morning. Speak for him, Luke."

I went to my father from the prison and asked him to release Peter. It was not because of my aunt's plea. (She had only made this to me as a last resort; she had asked to see my father but he had refused.) Except in her reminder that Peter had saved me from the polyboar. By speaking for him now I could cancel that debt and make us quits.

My father listened in silence then, but ordered Peter's release the next day, as soon as the burning was over. I did not go to see it. My father did, and sat, I was told, like stone.

It was not a long one; he had made sure of that. The people cheered, for his safety and the destruction of his enemy. The only trouble came from the Christians. They opposed the taking of life, even in battle or the execution of murderers, and always made a nuisance of themselves on such occasions. The people pelted them with filth and abused them. And one who called the Prince a murderer was taken by the guards. He was tried later but only condemned to the stocks for a day. The Christians, it was well known, were all mad, and no one took them seriously.

six

The Machines of Petersfield

It was a wretched winter. The palace was a place of gloom, ruled by a man who did not smile but drank greatly in an endeavor to forget what would not be forgotten. The heaviness of the atmosphere, so strong a contrast with the lightness that my mother's presence had engendered, of itself kept her in mind. And the weather was in tune with all this. Day after day the blizzards raged, until it was impossible for the polymufs to clear the streets and snow packed higher and higher against the walls of the houses: people had to cut steps down to their doors. It was impossible to exercise the horses who grew vicious in their stables. We could not exercise ourselves either, and turned stale and sour from the lack. The Christmas Feast was held as usual and my father took his place at the head of the long table. But there was little enough cheer. It was said that Christmas had started as a Christian business, celebrating the birth of their god, and this year one could believe it; it was so dreary a time. The polymuf jugglers and clowns, the musicians, had no occupation. My father saw to it that they did not go hungry but they were unhappy, not being able to use their gifts and gain applause. In the new year, when the weather held clear for a week, many of them left the city for more promising courts.

Martin and Edmund and I quarreled often enough during this drab confining time, but we remained friends. I cannot speak for their feelings but I had great need of them, with my father withdrawn into a private misery, and my own thoughts wretched enough. Strangely, the impulse to go to the house in the River Road, an impulse which had disappeared in the summer and autumn, came back now at intervals, quite unexpectedly. Doing some ordinary thing, I would think of going there, hearing my aunt's sharp voice bidding me wipe my feet, sitting down to dinner at the little table in the poky room. Then I would remember that all this was past, and how it had ended, and would feel a pain like the twisting of a knife in my chest. The pain went quicker if the others were by.

And Edmund was more willing to come to the palace than he had been. It was as though what had happened dissolved his resentments. My father, as anyone could see by looking at him, had paid a heavy penalty for becoming Prince. I don't think Edmund took any joy in this. He had changed from a hatred of him, which could not be hidden even though unexpressed, to a different feeling, almost one of admiration.

He said one day, about Peter:

"Does he ever visit your father, Luke?"

I said truthfully: "My father receives few visitors."

"But Peter?"

"No."

He had not been to the palace since his release. I myself had seen him once or twice in the Citadel, going about his duties as Captain, but we had not spoken. Edmund said:

"He was fortunate."

I had not spoken to them or anyone about my meeting with my aunt and my plea to my father for Peter. I doubted, in any case, whether my words had turned a scale. My father's circle of affection was small and he had lost two from it already; he would not have wished to forfeit a third unless it were forced on him.

I said: "He had no part in it."

"There are some who think differently. He usually slept in the palace, but not that night."

"Because he was on duty in the Citadel. My aunt knew that."

"And I've heard it said he was against questioning the polymuf, insisting he was a madman who had acted on his own."

"I was there," I said. "It was a remark, no more. It meant nothing and there was no insisting."

We were in the east wing of the palace, in a parlor on the

first floor. It was a part that had been left empty and unpainted for many years. The walls were dingy and cracked: Strohan, the palace butler, had asked my father if he should set the polymufs to decorating them but had been told no. Edmund and I were playing chess. Martin, who in any case was too good for either of us, was reading a book. He looked up from it, and said:

"The city is full of rumors. Being penned in, people have nothing to do but talk."

"And mostly nonsense," I said.

"Yet it is worth listening to it," Edmund said. "Even if it is nonsense, it is often useful to know what kind of nonsense men believe."

I accepted that, surprised only that he should have said it. But he had changed in the past months, as we all had. He thought more, and more deeply. And although we were friends I knew I did not have all the secrets of his mind, any more than he had mine.

Martin said: "People even say he is turning Christian."

I asked in surprise: "Peter?"

"He has been seen with them."

"If he does," Edmund said, "you are safe, Luke. Christians may not kill, and so he could not take revenge."

"Revenge?" I asked. "For what?"

"For a mother burned in the market square. It is not something one forgets. They say your father is a fool to have spared him. I don't think so. I think he knows his own strength. He is like a dog I once saw come into a pack that were snarling and fighting. The pack made way for him and when he turned his back on them, though together they could have fallen on him and killed him, they dared not even show their teeth. But you may need to take more care."

"I can look after myself."

"Still, if he turns Christian it makes it easier. And he would have to give up his Captaincy."

"That shows what moonshine it is! He would never surrender his sword."

Martin, while we were talking, had left his book and strolled restlessly about the room. He stopped in front of a picture which hung on the wall. It was very old and showed animals in cages, but like no animals we had ever seen. There was one that was tawny in color, shaped something like a cat but with a mane behind its head; and judging by the size of a man in the picture at least a hundred times bigger than any cat could be. Another, roughly resembling a man, was hideously ugly with receding head and chin, hairy and tailed. And near the cages a second man walked what might have been a horse except that it was covered with black and white stripes.

Martin said: "This must be from before the Disaster. And yet they say that the polymufs, both beasts and men, only came after the Disaster, as a punishment for the wickedness of our Ancestors."

"It may not be from before the Disaster," Edmund said. "We don't know how old it is."

"But there are polymuf beasts in it, full grown, and men with them, so in any case something is wrong."

"They may be only the imaginings of a painter," I suggested.

"They don't look like imaginings."

Edmund said: "Take it to Ezzard and ask him."

"He would destroy it probably. I should think it has only survived because no Seer has noticed it."

"Take care when you speak of the Seer," Edmund said, "or you will never be accepted as an Acolyte."

The joke was long threadbare but we all laughed. We needed something to laugh at.

One day, during the period of easier weather, the time when the clowns and musicians and jugglers were leaving the city, the thought of the house in the River Road came on me again, a joy and a pain together. I was on my own in the lower part of the city, below the Buttercross. I had been meaning to go across the river to the Armory but on the impulse I changed my direction. I walked the familiar street where I had not been for so long. The polymufs had cleared the High Street of snow but here it still lay, packed in the center, at the sides drifted against the houses. I came to her house and stared at it. Steps had been cut before this door as before the rest, and smoke rose from the chimney. I wondered who lived there now, but I did not care. The journey had done me no good; I would have been better staying away.

I turned to go and found him almost on me: the snow had muffled his footsteps. We looked at each other, for the first time really since the fire, and I saw the deeper lines in his face, the marks of grief and long brooding. He said:

"Health, Luke. You have come to see me?"

I said stupidly: "To see you? Here? You live here?"

"Why not? It is my home."

As we both knew, he had left it last summer to join my father in the palace, at the time when Aunt Mary refused the offer of a bigger house. I had assumed that from the palace he had gone to live in the Lines, with the other unmarried Captains.

I said: "You have no woman to tend you."

"I have the maids."

"Polymufs . . ."

He shrugged. "They see to things."

It was unheard of for a man, except sometimes when bereaved and old, to live without human care and companionship, of wife, mother, sister—some womanly relation. It showed how badly he had taken things that he should do so; and made the notion of him turning Christian just a little less incredible. But even apart from the solitariness, how could he bear to go on living with such memories as the house must continually call to mind? I found it bad enough to have to look at the snow-topped ruins of the palace's north wing. To be in the house—listen to the ticking of the clock she wound each night, look at the plants in pots of which she had been so proud—was to seek pain which anyone in his right mind would shun.

While I hesitated, trying to think of something to say, he said:

"Are you coming in?"

"No. I have ... someone to see."

We looked at each other. I do not know what he thought —that I had come to gloat, perhaps—but I knew there was nothing I could say which would bridge the chasm between us. We called each other cousin, and in fact were half brothers. We had been friends. We could not become strangers. It left only one thing: we must be enemies.

Winter ended at last in a thaw accompanied by rain storms which made the river flood its banks; the waters rose at one point to lap against the block of stone in the High Street which still carried the broken legs of what had been a statue—of a great Prince of ancient times, it was said. But when the rains stopped and the west wind died away there was fitful sunlight and everywhere the trees began to bud, bursting into green as though to make up for time lost.

It was the Spring Fair again, and the Contest. Not a good one: the favorite was Mark Greene and he won without much difficulty and took the jeweled sword. I sat with the spectators, my own sword hanging from my belt, and heard people talk about how much better the Contest had been last year. They said flattering things and I made awkward replies. Later Edmund, who had sat with me, said:

"One would think you did not like praise, you receive it so awkwardly."

"I like the thought of it," I said, "but the reality makes me uneasy."

He smiled. "You must learn to overcome that. Or at least not to show it."

"Praise is worth having from a few. Those whose judgment one values."

"And if *I* tell you it was a better Contest last year?"

We laughed. I said: "And would have been better still with a different ending?"

"True enough!" He paused. "If I had not underrated you as I did . . . I fought it over in my mind often enough afterward and knew I could have beaten you. I would have liked a second chance."

"There are no second chances."

"Not in the Contest, I agree."

"Not in anything that matters."

He shook his head. "I will not accept that, Luke. I will never accept it."

It was at this time that my father roused himself from the torpor which had held him for so many months. Orders were given and obeyed. The ruins of the north wing were cleared away by polymufs, and after them came builder dwarfs and there was sawing of wood and hammering of nails all day. Others worked on the rest of the palace, mending and cleaning and painting.

Nor was that the end of the city's new activity. The dwarfs were also busy in the Armory and at harness-making. People had said that with the Prince sunk in melancholy there would be no fighting this year. Now they knew differently. He still did not smile but he seemed possessed by a fury that drove him toward action. He was up at daybreak and busy all day making preparations for the campaign. In the middle of April the army rode out to the southwest.

I rode with them. Not, it is true, as a warrior, though I wore my sword, but as assistant to the Sergeant in charge of the camp followers. These were the men who looked after the Prince and the Captains in the field, putting up tents, seeing to equipment, cooking and so on. It was work which in the city would have been done by polymufs but no army took polymufs with it even as menials. These were men unfit for one reason or another to be warriors but glad enough to go with the army, for pickings or maybe just for the excitement. They were a rough lot and unruly when they were in drink but the Sergeant, a gray-bearded man called Burke, with a limp that came from an old sword wound, ruled them well.

We made up a baggage train, the gear loaded on carts pulled by mules. We did not always take the same route as the army—the mules were sure-footed but the carts themselves could not always go where horses could. It was particularly true on this campaign, for we were riding against Petersfield which lay in a fold on the far side of the Downs. The ground to be traversed was hilly and often rough. We made our way to appointed places and worked hard, having a longer road to travel.

I learned a lot, from the best way of sleeping on hard ground with only a single blanket to keep out the cold to the techniques of killing and skinning and jointing a bullock: once we were out of our own territory we lived, as raiding armies always did, on the land we were invading. I had thought myself fit but soon became much fitter. My hands were first sore then calloused from the labors of mule-driving, loading and unloading, hauling on ropes to free carts whose wheels were stuck in the mud. I wished often enough that I could be with the main body of the army, riding high up across the shoulder of a hill while we struggled along beneath them, but this at any rate was better than being left with the garrison in the city.

Our boundary followed the river as far north as West Meon. It was there the army crossed, taking the broader southerly route through the Downs, and I looked on foreign fields for the first time in my life. They seemed no different from our own, growing wheat and potatoes, very few with cattle. (Dairy farming was for the most part carried on in parts closer to the cities, where the beasts were not so vulnerable to raiders.) We passed through a hamlet less than a mile inside the border. Its single street was empty, the windows tight shuttered on the houses, silent except for a dog barking somewhere out of sight. But we knew that eyes would be watching us, and that the pigeons would be in flight, carrying word of our coming to Petersfield.

The battle took place a week later and I saw it all. We had come up from cultivated land to higher ground cropped by sheep and halted. We had a spring-fed stream with a good head of water and the sheep kept us in fresh meat. My father waited for the Prince of Petersfield to meet him. The scouts brought news of his coming one drab gray morning with a chill east wind driving gusts of rain in our faces.

Our camp was in the lee of a rounded hill topped by a clump of trees, like our own St. Catherine's. I told Burke I wanted to go up there to watch.

He said: "If you like, Master. I've seen enough fights in my time but you're young enough to have the appetite."

"You don't need to come with me."

He shook his head. "I'm to see you safe home, if things go wrong. And that's not easy. The rats may lie quiet in their holes while you go through in advance, but they come out with their teeth sharpened for anyone straggling back."

He saw that our haversacks were well supplied with rations and our canteens filled with water. The Spirits, through Ezzard, had prophesied victory for Winchester, a greater one than last year's, but as he said, an old soldier might believe in the Spirits but was not such a fool as to trust his life to them. If our army were scattered the baggage train would be lost and it was difficult enough escaping through hostile territory without going hungry and thirsty as well. We led our horses up the hill and tethered them in the grove of trees. The wind howled through, shaking the branches, but the rain had stopped. Then, our cloaks wrapped tightly round us, we looked down and watched the armies come together.

It was a slow business at first. Our army, more than five hundred men on horseback, stood grouped about the blue and gold standard, near which I picked out the tall figure of my father on Guinea, his helmet topped by the royal spike. The Petersfield men came on slowly from the east, in a wedge formation with their Prince and his standard, all green, deep inside the wedge. From time to time they stopped. The taunts and jeers from both sides came up to us, thin, tiny like the figures. At one time I exclaimed as the enemy appeared to turn tail, but Burke shook his head. It was part of the ritual, he explained, and no retreat but a show of scorn, meaning they held us in such contempt that they could expose their backs.

"If we attacked now . . ."

"It would be to give them best in that."

"But we might win."

"We might. If you can call it a victory, achieved without honor."

I said: "We face the wind."

"It blows from their city."

"But if we had held the ridge on the right—they could only have come at us across wind, and uphill also. Or would that be dishonorable, too?"

He laughed. "Not that I have heard. But your father is a strong fighter rather than a canny one. He thinks he needs no such aid."

"But if *they* had taken the ridge . . ."

"It would have made things harder for us. Watch! It begins, I think."

The two forces were riding to a clash with growing momentum. My hands were clenched and I felt the nails score my palms. The wedge advanced toward our ragged line and as it drove in I saw swords flashing even in this dull air. Our line, giving way at the center, curved round to embrace their flanks. Then it was a melee, impossible to sort out except by reference to the swaying standards, confusion to eyes and ears alike. The din, though distant, was awful: shouts and cries of men, screams of horses, rattle and clash of swords.

The fight lasted for three quarters of an hour. Then slowly the sides disentangled as the Petersfield men fell back. The green standard bobbed away on a retreating tide.

"Is it over?" I asked. "Have we won?"

"We have won this fight," Burke said. "I think there will be others. They gave way in too good order to be ready to ask for peace."

"If we have beaten them once we can beat them again."

"True enough. Except that next time they will be closer in to their own city."

"What difference does that make?"

"An army fights harder the nearer it is to home."

But they did not stand in our path again. We took East Meon and moved on, downhill at last to the low ground in which Petersfield itself stood, west of the Rother River. We camped under their walls, out of arrow shot, and waited for them either to sue for peace or come out to fight us. We were among their home farms and had food enough. They must do something or their harvest would be lost.

Pickets were set at night, though an attack was unlikely then. Darkness favors the defenders provided they are prepared; we had stakes and ditches ready. Then one morning, as the sky was beginning to grow light in the east, I awoke to what I thought was the crash of thunder. While I was still struggling to my senses I heard another crash, and shouts of pain. I pulled on my boots and got to my feet to find the camp in confusion. There was a third crash. It was different from thunder and in any case the sky was full of high thin cloud. I looked toward the city and saw, just before the next crash, a red flare of light from the walls.

Gradually some order emerged. The Sergeants rallied the men. I went to my father's tent and found him there with his Captains. One said:

"I have heard of these things. They throw metal a great distance. But they are machines. The Seers forbid them."

Harding said: "They bark more than they bite. Two men wounded, I am told."

"So far," another said. "But if they keep on with this long enough . . ."

Harding said: "We can move the camp back. I don't know what range they have but it must have limits. And we are still in their lands."

"Once we retreat it will give them heart. And if they bring these machines with them . . . if we ride against thunder that belches steel, will the men still follow?"

Harding shrugged. "We have no choice but to retreat. We could leave this campaign and ride against Alton again, or south to Chichester."

Blaine, a red-faced burly man with small sharp eyes, said: "What does the Prince say?"

Neither he nor Harding would be sorry to see the campaign against Petersfield called off. It might not bring my father down but it would besmirch the reputation he had gained last year and help undermine his power. I saw them watching him.

My father said: "They use machines. It is not just the Seers but the Spirits that forbid them."

"They can kill for all that."

"The Spirits promised us victory," my father said. "And these men defy them. So we attack."

Harding said: "How, since they will not come out?"

"We attack the city."

They stared at him in disbelief. One of the reasons Stephen had been laughed at, building his walls higher each year, was that in more than a generation no city in the civilized lands had fallen to the army of another. Taunton had gone down, three years before, but Taunton was a border city and the barbarians from the west had taken it. The armies fought, harder, as Burke had said, the nearer they were to home, and won or lost, and peace was made, ransoms and tributes paid; but the cities stayed safe and untouched. What my father was saying sounded not merely foolhardy but almost heretical.

Blaine said, his tone only just concealing the sneer:

"And take it? All the easier, do you think, for having the machines against us? They may or may not be able to bring them against us in the field. But, by the Great, we know they are on the battlements. Are we to walk like flies up the walls and into their very mouths?"

"Why not?" my father said. "Since the Spirits are with us."

There was a silence and I saw the Captains look at one

another. If one spoke up in opposition the rest might rally to him. But it was my cousin Peter who spoke. He said:

"Why not? When the Prince leads, do his Captains fear to follow?"

It seemed hopeless. They had to advance on foot, with the machines, three of them, blasting down at them from above. Even without these, scaling the walls would have seemed impossible. Because of the risk of earthquakes they were of loose construction but they were steeply sloping and more than thirty feet high, manned by archers who could pick off the crawling attackers with ease. One of the Captains had suggested making the attack at some other point where there might not be machines, but my father refused. We went under the Spirits' protection and would advance against the machines whose use the Spirits forbade.

I watched from the camp with Burke. The machines roared again and again and I saw our men fall as the hot steel slashed their bodies. They were in bow range, too, now and the arrows also took their toll. My father led them. I do not think they would have gone forward against such odds under any other Captain. If he fell, they would scatter and run, and I guessed the enemy's fire would be concentrated on him. Even if, by a miracle, he went on unscathed, I thought they must break as comrades dropped and died at their sides.

Then the greater miracle happened. From the central machine came another roar but louder, more shattering, and the wall around and underneath it exploded outward. Dots darted through the air, of rock, of metal, of the limbs and bodies of men. As the dust and debris settled one could see that the wall was breached. At that point it was no more than a pile of rubble with a gap of ten feet or more at the top, and undefended.

There was a shout from the men of Winchester and they moved forward faster, running and stumbling upward over the rocky slope. Then they were through the gap and inside the city.

SEVEN

The High Seers

That year we had strange and distinguished guests at the Autumn Fair: the High Seers came to the city.

They came, three of them, black-cloaked on pure white horses, and the city turned out to greet them at the North Gate. It was not a greeting such as had been given to the army when we returned with the spoils of Petersfield. Then the people had shouted their acclamations for the Prince and his followers, and even I, riding with Burke at the head of the camp followers, had heard my name echo from the city's walls. The High Seers were received in silence, but a silence that was perhaps more impressive than any noise, having reverence in it.

The crazy Christians on one side, there had been always some who were skeptical concerning the Spirits, and Ezzard's powers as mediator and interpreter of their will.

Many, possibly a majority, contrived to hold belief and disbelief in dubious balance. There was something there, they thought, but they did not quite know what, or what the extent and limitations of its authority might be. I think I was among them. Even though I had been angry with Martin for expressing blasphemy, it had been chiefly through anxiety over men's response to it, not fear of what the Spirits might do. In part I believed in the Spirits—after all, they had named my father Prince and myself his heir, a Prince to be—in part, I doubted.

But it was hard for any to go on doubting after the fall of Petersfield. My father, calling on the Spirits for aid, had led his men in an attack against walls which, strong in themselves, carried also diabolical machines capable of throwing death from great distances: the camp, on which steel first fell, had been almost half a mile away. If there were no Spirits, or they had no power to help, the project was ridiculous, scarcely sane. But the Spirits had shown their presence and their strength, destroying the machine at the very moment that it belched out death, and by that destruction opening a way for our men to pour through and overcome the shocked and demoralized defenders.

In thankfulness my father had decreed the building of a new Seance Hall, three times the size of the old one. The High Seers were come to consecrate its foundation, and the city greeted them in awe. Each city had its Seer, with his attendant Acolytes, but the High Seers had always stayed in their Sanctuary beyond Salisbury, the holy place. There, it was said, they communicated with the Spirits not just fitfully, for an hour at a time, as Ezzard did, but continuously, even passing through from our substantial world to that strange invisible plane in which the Spirits had their being. It was wonderful that they should have left the Sanctuary and come so far, thirty-five miles at least, to honor us.

That evening the High Seers sat at the long table in the Great Hall, on my father's right hand. Facing them were other Seers: Ezzard and the Seers of Petersfield and Romsey. It was a great concentration of holiness and the banquet was not, at first at any rate, as banquets usually are, noisy with jests and rowdy laughter. Men ate and drank in a solemn hush; heads turned at the sudden squeaking of a chair, reproving the one who sat there.

The Seers ate and drank sparingly, the High Seers eating least of all. I heard it whispered that the little they took was only for politeness' sake, that usually they supped on the food of the Spirits that could be neither touched nor seen by ordinary people. Whatever their customary food was it plainly nourished them; they themselves were solid enough and one at least, sitting between the other two, was big indeed and amply stomached.

They left the table before the sweets were brought and all, my father included, stood in respect as they walked together from the Hall. When they had gone there was a kind of sigh that rippled down the line of guests, followed by noisy chatter that burst out in relief. The clowns came with the sweets, and serving maids filled the pots with the strong dark brew of ale, itself sweet to the tongue, which was drunk after meat. I took some myself but only sipped it. I had seen enough heads fuddled with ale to be careful in drinking. I could never see what pleasure men got from being made silly and stupid by it. To me it was a hateful thing not to have control of one's mind and body.

My father swallowed down his pot and called for another but he had a good head for liquor: even when drinking heavily he never seemed to me the worse for it. Tonight, after his second pot, he rose. The guests that remained rose also but he bade them sit down and continue with their feast; he was excusing himself because he had things to attend to. He left, as they toasted him yet again: Prince of Winchester, conqueror of Petersfield! Not long after a servant came to me quietly. My father wanted to see me in his private room.

I found him sitting in the old wooden armchair. His boots were off and he was toasting his feet at the fire. He nodded as I came in and bobbed my head to him.

"Sit down, Luke. I hope you don't mind that I took you from the feast."

I said: "No, sir."

"You are young still but there are things about which I would like to talk with you. Partly because they are your concern as well as mine." He shrugged. "And partly, I suppose, because there is no one else to say them to."

In the past there had been my mother, who would smile, half listening, and tell him she was sure that everything he did was right, and would succeed because he did it. And my aunt, who would comment more shrewdly. And Peter.

Peter had spoken up for him before the walls of Winchester and gained great glory in the battle that followed, fighting with a reckless courage that everyone praised. But I knew he could not talk to Peter any more than I could—could not look at him without remembering that which he wished with all his heart to forget. There was Wilson, but old and trusted colleague as he was, some things could not be said to him.

I waited. He said:

"I saw your face when I spoke to the Captains before the attack on the walls. Did you think me mad, son?"

"Why, no, sir..."

He shook his head impatiently. "Or reckless, or what you will. At any rate, you thought we could not succeed. As the others did. They came with me because I shamed them into doing so. None of you had faith in the Spirits."

I began to speak again and again he bore me down.

"Let us talk about faith," he said. "It is a strange thing. Before you have faith you must believe, and before you believe there must be evidence of some sort to persuade the mind. Faith is remembering that evidence and holding to it against all that seems to challenge or contradict it. And some evidences are stronger than others, and more important. I have faith that my dinner will be brought to me tomorrow, but not such faith that I would sit long at an empty table."

He paused. I was not sure if he wanted me to say something and anyway had nothing to say. He went on slowly:

"You know what my mood was last winter, and you

know the reasons for it. I think I went on living because it was too much trouble to seek death. Ezzard tried to give me comfort, telling me that your mother was a Spirit now, with the other Spirits, that she lived still in their world and that one day I would meet her again. He brought me messages that he said came from her. There was no comfort in them. Time after time I sent him away.

"Then at last, as winter ended, he persuaded me to visit him in the Seance Hall. None knew of it and no other was present, not even an Acolyte. Just the Seer and I. And there, in the darkness, I heard her voice. She talked to me, in human speech."

He looked at me and his face lightened into a smile, so rare now.

"I do not ask you to believe this because you did not hear it, and a man can be deceived by his ears. But I *know* I was not deceived. I could never mistake that voice. I heard her speak."

I asked: "What did she say, sir?"

"That she was well, that I must not brood over losing her, that we would meet again. It was not what she said but that she said it. I knew then that Ezzard had told me the truth: that there was a world of Spirits and she was in it.

"There is still more. Before I led the army against Petersfield, Ezzard told me how things would go. He said they would fight us in the field and then retire behind their walls. He said their Prince was a man who defied the Spirits, who had found old machines of war and would use them.

So I was not surprised when thunder broke from their walls that morning. He said if we fought against them we would win."

He looked a long time at Margry's painting of my mother which hung on the wall opposite his chair. It showed her smiling, a shaft of sunlight on her hair and face, puppies in a basket at her feet and flowers behind her head: accompanied by all the things she loved best. He said:

"One thing Ezzard did not promise me: that I myself would come back safe. He did not say I would not, but I thought that was his meaning. He spoke strongly of the need to protect you, my heir. But perhaps it was my own desire that misled me there. Because to die in such a way, fighting on behalf of the Spirits, must mean that I would join her, at once, in the Spirit world."

He hunched back in his chair, letting his shoulders droop, and for the first time I saw him as old, a man with a burden in which there was now no trace of joy.

"All happened as Ezzard foretold. And I returned in triumph, and I do not think either the Blaines or Hardings will trouble us in the future. I do not know how many years I have to live"—he spoke as a man contemplating a long and wearisome journey—"but when I die the people will call for a Perry to succeed a Perry. You will be Prince of this city. It is something else Ezzard has told us, at the bidding of the Spirits, but even without their aid it would be so. And because you are the Prince in Waiting, I have another thing to tell you. Ezzard has spoken to me about Petersfield. It is the wish of the Spirits that we do not exact ransom but annex this city, making it and all its lands part of our realm of Winchester."

Despite what he had already told me, I was astonished. The cities were the cities, individual and sovereign. One might defeat another in war and take tribute, outlying land perhaps, as we had done from Alton, but at the end of each campaign the armies withdrew behind their own walls.

I asked: "Is it possible?"

"The Spirits command it."

"But will the men of Petersfield accept? Or will you keep an army there all winter?"

"If necessary; but it will not be necessary. Their Seer agrees with Ezzard on this. He will proclaim it to them and his power is great since their city was taken through defiance of the Spirits. I shall appoint one of their own Captains as my lieutenant. The Seer of Petersfield has given me good advice on choosing him."

The Seers, it seemed, were taking a larger hand in our affairs: much larger. I was not sure I cared for it. But it was true they spoke for the Spirits and that the Spirits had showed their powers. True also that so far their powers had been exercised to our benefit. It would not be wise to offend them.

I was at Edmund's house on the day the proclamation about Petersfield was made. It was his mother's birthday and I had taken her a present, a set of pink ribbons made up into a shape something like a rose, to pin on a dress. As soon as I gave it to her I realized I had made a mistake. It was the sort of frivolous thing which would have suited my mother but Edmund's mother had been, even as the Prince's Lady, a homely woman not given to fripperies, and now was content to dress dowdily in browns and dark blues. It occurred to me that choosing a rose shape made things worse. Her one great joy when she lived in the palace had been the rose garden. I think it was the only thing of luxury she missed when she went to live on Salt Street. The present might remind her of it; she might even think I had meant it to.

She thanked me warmly but I was embarrassed and uneasy. My mood was not improved by Edmund's sister, who was also there. She was a year older than Edmund, a thin, sharp-tongued girl. I was never, at the best of times, at ease with girls, but those who used sarcasm bothered me even more than the ones who giggled together in corners. She said something now about the gift I had brought, which I did not fully understand but which sounded mocking. Then she spoke about the proclamation. What a great Prince I would be one day. Who knew how many more cities my father might not conquer?

"Who knows?" I said. "Maybe Romsey, too. If so, I will bring you a gift from there. A lily, perhaps."

I saw her thin face flush. She had been betrothed to the son of Romsey's Prince but this had been annulled, of course, following her father's deposition and death. Lilies were what brides carried at their weddings. She said:

"I know one thing you will never bring to any lady: that is courtesy. It requires breeding, and if you become Prince of all the cities in the world you will always lack that."

Her words cut like knives, reducing me to tongue-tied silence. Her mother intervened, saying:

"That will do, Jenny. You have been teasing him."

"Does a gentleman insult a lady, even if he is teased?"

"It has nothing to do with that," her mother said. "Some men are at ease with womenfolk, some not. You know Luke is of the latter, and you should not provoke him."

I said: "I am sorry, ma'am."

She smiled. "I know you are."

Then Edmund came in with Charles, whose arm was still in a sling from a wound he had got at Petersfield. She turned to them, smiling again, but the smile was different. It transformed her plain face into great beauty. I had never seen such a look as that in my mother's face. They grinned back at her, and I knew where Edmund had gained the strength to overcome his disappointments and resentment. I was jealous of him.

It was near dinner time. They asked me to stay and share the meal with them but my awkwardness, the consciousness of having put myself in the wrong, was so great that I refused. I realized, from the quick look of scorn Jenny gave me, that I had made things worse. She thought, and probably so did the others, that I was refusing out of a feeling of superiority.

I knew that was not true but could do nothing to remedy it. I was in a black mood as I walked away down Salt Street. It was not superiority, I insisted to myself, but awkwardness. And jealousy? I did not want to look at that. I went back to dinner at the palace and my father and I sat opposite each other in silence. His thoughts these days were far away except when he was concerned with war or statesmanship. And my gloom continued, no less oppressive for being a condition to which I was well accustomed. I expected it would last all day, and it did.

Before the High Seers left the city I was called to private audience. Ezzard took me to them in a parlor of his house behind the Seance Hall. From the window one could see the workmen, dwarfs and men, busy on the new Hall which was already beginning to rise beside the old one. My eyes, though, were on the High Seers whom I was seeing for the first time at close quarters.

My neck, as I made obeisance to them, prickled with unease. I reminded myself that they would not harm me: I had not, as far as I knew, offended the Spirits and my father had been highly favored by them. I had been summoned in good will. And yet my flesh crawled as the chief High Seer, a small, very wrinkled man, his face spotted brown with age, held out his hand for me to kiss the ring on his little finger. It was a band of gold, set with seven emeralds: Ezzard's ring had only a single green stone in it. These were the great ones, the true familiars and servants of the Spirits. Even though I knew they wished me well, I feared them.

"So you are Luke," he said, "the Prince in Waiting, heir to Winchester and Petersfield."

"Yes, sire."

"You have learned your catechism from Ezzard? Tell me, boy, what are the Spirits?"

"They are of two kinds, sire: the Spirits of Men, and the Eternals."

"Describe them."

"The Spirits of Men are those who have lived on earth. Their duty is to watch over their descendants who are still in the body. They are the lower order. The higher order is the Eternals, who have always been, will always be. Both orders serve the Great Spirit whose name and being are a mystery."

"What is the duty of man?"

"To obey the commands of the Great Spirit in all things."

"How is a man to know these commands?"

"They are revealed by the Spirits through the Seers."

He nodded, bobbing his head, and I saw a little of the bare head under the black cowl, the skin smooth and taut in contrast to the wrinkled face.

"Well enough. Are the Spirits good or evil?"

I hesitated. It was not an easy question and not among those in the catechism which one answered by rote. I said:

"Some seem evil to men whom they punish. But it is men's wickedness that is at fault. The Spirits only do the Great Spirit's bidding."

"And is the Great Spirit good or evil?"

The catechism came to my aid again. "He is beyond good and evil. He is, and all things serve him."

"And you, Luke, do you obey the Spirits and worship the Great Spirit?"

"Yes, sire."

"The Spirits are good to those who serve them. Like

your father. They have rewarded him well. Is that not so?"

I thought of him as he had been when he was no more than a Captain, remembering his laugh which had seemed to come from deep in the belly, and as I had seen him that morning, silent in his chair staring at the picture on the wall. But it was true he had been given wealth and power, rule over not just one city but two. And he himself made no complaint against the Spirits.

I nodded. The High Seer said:

"Remember this always. All men are serfs to the Spirits, but they choose some to fulfill their will in special ways. Your father is such, and you are another. The Spirits have a mission for you to perform."

I asked, curiosity overcoming my unease: "What is that, sire?"

"It is not time for it to be revealed. But the time will come. And when it does you must obey, unhesitatingly, with all your heart and soul. Do you promise this?"

"Yes, sire."

"You must obey whatever the orders may be. Some will seem strange. Remember that while men are bound by the laws of the Spirits, the Spirits are bound only by the commands of the Great Spirit himself. They can change the laws they have made if that seems good to them."

"I will remember, sire."

"Good. Your destiny is a great one. The Spirits will aid you but much depends on yourself. We are glad to have seen you, and that you promise well. We take good news back to the Sanctuary."

If the Seers knew all things and they were such intimates of the Spirits, I did not see that they could take back any news that was not known already. Perhaps, though, it was not meant literally but just as a vague commendation for my having made the right responses. I kissed his hand again before I left, and the hands of the other High Seers. The big one I had noticed at the feast looked bigger than ever, like an over-prosperous farmer, and I wondered again that he could nourish such a bulk on Spirits' food. To my amazement he smiled at me.

"Are you a swordsman, Luke?"

I said cautiously: "I have learned sword play, and am still learning."

"You will have a sword to be proud of one day. A sword of the Spirits." I suppose I looked uncertain, and he went on: "No, but a real one—tougher and harder and sharper than anything the dwarfs can make. A sword for a Prince of Princes." He smiled again. "We go back to see to the forging of it."

I was to meet Edmund and Martin afterward. They asked me how it had gone and I told them some of what had passed, but nothing of the talk of great destinies or a sword of the Spirits. Edmund said:

"The usual mumbo jumbo, in fact. It is a pity, since the Spirits have such great powers, that they talk such rubbish."

I did not chide him for blaspheming, as I had once chided Martin. I knew that, half believing in the Spirits, he wholly hated them; that remained even though he was now apparently reconciled to what had happened, to my father's being Prince and me his heir. I was sorry that he took such risks but knew that argument would only make him worse. I expected Martin to say something less positive but indicating a measure of agreement: they infected each other in this. To my surprise, he said:

"I saw a Seer today also. Not a High Seer. Only Ezzard."

I asked: "Why?"

"I am to be an Acolyte."

"You're joking!"

That was Edmund, incredulous. Martin said:

"No, it's true."

"You mean—you believe all this, you want to spend your life praying to the Spirits? Because a machine blew up and Luke's father took Petersfield instead of getting himself killed and his army scattered as should have happened?"

"No," Martin said, "because I want to find out."

"Find out what?"

"The truth about the Spirits. Whatever it is, the Seers must know it."

"And if there's nothing to find out?"

He smiled. "Well, I'll know *that*, won't I?"

"Will you tell us?"

"Perhaps."

I said sharply: "An Acolyte is bound by deep oaths. If he breaks them his life is forfeit, and in torture."

Martin smiled again. "Or perhaps not. It depends."

"You should not talk like that. It is dangerous even to have such thoughts."

They both laughed. Edmund said:

"Poor Luke, you must remember he takes his Spirits very seriously. And why not? Perhaps we would if they looked after us as well as they do him. Shall I turn Acolyte with you, Martin? I don't think so. I'd look an even bigger fool with a shaved head than you will."

Another thing happened before the Christmas Feast: my cousin Peter married. He married a girl from the Christians, whom he had still been seeing. But he did not become a Christian himself and his marriage caused no great stir. A woman's beliefs were not thought to be of much importance, and she was not one of the fanatical sort but a quiet, well-behaved girl. Not a beauty, either, but he seemed content with her.

It did not affect his standing with the other Captains, rather the reverse. With marriage his manner changed back to his old amiability and he was at his ease again and put them at theirs. To the reputation as a warrior he had gained in the summer was added popularity. He was thought a good fellow, no longer under the cloud of his mother's crime and execution.

But when my father offered him a house as a wedding gift he refused it, politely enough, saying he preferred to go on living on the River Road. And when he and I met, although we gave each other greetings, we did not stop to speak.

EiGHT

A HEAd ON
tHE EAST GATE

In December there was a state visit from Prince Jeremy of Romsey, in return for that of my father's which had been cut short a year before. He brought his eldest son with him, and they stayed for the Christmas Feast.

Prince Jeremy was a fattish, small, ineffectual-seeming man with a gingery mustache and beard, both delicately trimmed. His polymuf barber was one of the party and he spent an hour closeted with him each morning and came out oiled and scented. To my father he was deferential, almost obsequious, continually seeking his opinion and only offering his own when it was requested. In fact, his opinions were often worth having. Although he looked weak and effeminate his mind was shrewd.

The son, James, was a little older than I but a good deal taller and more adult in appearance; when he sometimes missed being shaved (as I think he did by design rather than accident or slovenliness) his chin was blue-stubbled with whiskers. I was astonished by his attitude to his father, which was one of condescension, almost of contempt, and by the father's acceptance of it.

To me he offered at first the same condescension. I made it clear that I would not stand for it, and his manner changed to a rather oily affability. I found that he followed me around; little as I cared for his company I could not without rudeness be rid of it for long. And it was not possible to be rude: this was a state visit and I had a duty to perform. I cut him short in his criticisms of his father but had to tolerate the rest of his whinings. He was envious of Winchester's wealth and prosperity and under cover of praising it continually bemoaned the poverty of his own city and of his father's palace. They had no painter to compare with Margry, their musicians were inferior, their buildings small and mean against ours—even the dogs no match for our Winchester breed. All this, with its barely concealed jealousy and resentment, was increasingly irritating as the days passed and I grew more and more familiar with his complaints.

But if it was bad enough having to endure his company on my own, it was worse when Martin and Edmund were there. Martin he practically ignored, except for a faint air of surprise that I should associate with a commoner. He gloated over Edmund. It was not done openly—there was no particular thing said to which one could take exception

—but there was no mistaking it. He had known Edmund, after all, as the Prince's son, and he was plainly delighted by the reversal in his fortunes and the family's present poverty.

Edmund for a time tolerated it, returning an equal but silent contempt which I think James was too stupid to notice. The break in his composure only came when one day in the street we met Edmund's sister, Jenny. She did not notice James right away and stopped to say something to her brother about a domestic matter: a drain at the house that needed unblocking. It was only after some moments that she saw James and her words faltered. Her face, already pricked to color by the frost in the air, crimsoned further.

James said, his voice cool and it seemed to me with an edge of mockery:

"Greetings, lady. We have met before, I believe."

The meeting, as we all knew, had been two years earlier and had been the occasion of their betrothal: the daughter of the Prince of Winchester and the heir to Romsey.

She said: "Yes, sir."

He smiled at her. "Should you ever come to Romsey, you must call on us."

The tone of insult was unmistakable. Their eyes met and his, in cruel arrogance, bore her gaze down. I had not thought I could be sorry for her but I was. She mumbled something and turned, walking away quickly over the packed snow. James called after her:

"Present my compliments to your lady mother." Jenny did not reply or look back. "Tell her I regret that I shall not be able to visit her in her new home."

Edmund, stung at last beyond endurance, started moving toward him, his fist doubling for a punch. I caught his arm and Martin did so from the other side. No provocation could be held to justify striking the son of a Prince who was a guest of the city: the offender must be charged and convicted and publicly lashed. James had seen his move and was smiling.

Edmund said: "Let me go. I'll . . ."

"No." I tightened my grip on his arm, making sure I hurt him. "It's not worth it." Our eyes locked. He was angry with me as well and I could see why. I said: "Go after Jenny. I'll see to this." He still struggled to get free. I whispered: "If you hit him, I must defend him. I have no choice. And then . . . do you want to have him watching while they take the lash to your naked back?"

He gave me a single look. I let go and he walked away. I motioned to Martin to go with him. James said:

"A pity you did not let him try."

I turned on him fiercely, so fiercely that he started back. I said:

"I did it for his sake, not yours. But if you insult a friend of mine in my presence again it will be I that cracks you, state visit or no state visit."

I walked away toward the palace. He followed, protesting that it was all an error: he had meant no insult. I did not answer. He caught up with me, and said:

"All the same, do you think you are wise to make a friend of such as him?"

I said sharply: "I do not need advice on choosing my friends."

He laughed, high and thin. "Of course! But I worry about you, Luke. You are too trusting."

I kept silent. I wanted no counsel from him, of any kind. Nor was it true. I knew myself well enough to know that with me trust was never constant but something which ebbed and flowed. I might trust a few in my good humor but when my mind was black clouded I trusted no one. This one, though, I would not trust under any conditions.

That evening, talking alone with my father, I asked how much longer they would stay. He said:

"Do you find that young James tries you?"

I gritted my teeth. "Almost beyond bearing."

He smiled. "I have noticed the effort you made and been proud of you for it. One can see why some lads are unpleasant—this one has ruled his father since he was in the cradle—but one does not dislike them less for the knowledge. But it may prove to have been worth it."

"I do not see how, sir."

"No, but I will tell you. The father is a soft man in some ways but at the same time cunning. He has been impressed by our success the last two summers. He realizes that we have the aid and blessing of the Spirits. He wants an alliance."

"For fear that we might attack him next?"

"In part, but not only through fear. He looks for advantages."

"What advantages?"

"This, like all things said in this room, is not to be spoken of." I nodded. "He proposes that next summer we join together in an attack on Andover."

Andover was due north of Romsey, about fifteen miles distant. The cities were old rivals but in recent years the northerners had been greatly the stronger. Romsey had paid much in tribute and yielded valuable land. I said:

"I can see why he wants our help. But there is not much honor for us in defeating Andover with Romsey's help."

"I felt the same. But there is more to it than honor. Or a shared ransom. Ambitions have grown all round since we took Petersfield. He says he can take Andover, as well."

"How?"

"There is a Sergeant in Andover who will see to it that one of the gates is opened. For a price."

"But that is treachery! There would be no honor . . ."

"Listen," my father said. "There are times when the world changes, when the customs of generations shatter and things are no longer fixed. Ezzard has told me we are in such a time. Because of this a man born a commoner became Prince of Winchester. Andrew of Petersfield used machines against us. We in turn took his city; and on the Spirits' command have kept it. The changes are not yet ended. If Prince of two cities, why not three?"

"But if Jeremy's army fights alongside ours, if it is he who has the key to the gates . . ."

"He is a timid man. He is shrewd enough but lacks courage. He is a little dog who wants a big dog to run with and will therefore let the big dog take what he wants and be content with the scraps. He offered me the city without my asking; he will be content with Stockbridge and the land around it. And with our friendship."

I said: "I can think of others I would sooner have as friends."

"So can I. But a Prince is bound by policy, not by liking. And by the Spirits. Ezzard supports this plan. He has told me: I will be Prince of many cities—you, if you are guided by the Spirits, Prince of all the cities in the land."

I was silent. I thought of asking: did we want such an empire? But I guessed the answer I would get—that our wanting or not wanting was unimportant. The Spirits required it. They had served us well so far but their wrath, if we failed them, could destroy us as quickly as their benevolence had raised us. We had no choice.

Edmund kept away for the remainder of the visit, and for a time after. In the end I sought him out at the house in Salt Street, and persuaded him to come with me to the stables. There were just the two of us. Martin was already under instruction to become an Acolyte and busy that morning.

We walked in silence at first. There was constraint between us, the recollection of our last parting. In the end I said:

"I am sorry for holding you back. I would have liked to see you hit him. I would have liked to hit him myself."

He did not reply at once and I thought he was still resentful. Then he said:

"No, you were right. It would not have been worth it to knock him down. What a toad he is! You would not believe how he fawned on me . . . in the old days."

I said feelingly: "I think I would believe it."

"And Jenny—he paid her such elaborate compliments and told her all the time how unworthy he was of her. It was true enough, but you could see he didn't believe it. She hated him even then but of course had to obey our father. If there is a consolation in what happened it is that the city is rid of that alliance."

I thought of what my father had told me but was silent. Edmund went on:

"She was saying, after that meeting, that she had only just realized what an escape she had in not having to marry him. She can marry whom she likes now, or not marry if she so wishes. There are advantages in no longer being royal. I would have had to marry for policy, too, and I would have detested it."

I said: "Does it matter so much? There are more important things."

"Do you think so?"

"One does not spend all that much time in the company of women. There is riding and hunting, battle, gaming— the company of one's fellow men."

Edmund shook his head. "It would matter to me." He

grinned, at last open and friendly again. "It is just as well that you do not mind, since you are going to have to obey the rules. As a matter of fact, Jenny and I were speculating the other day as to who was most likely to be the lady of the Prince of Princes. We were for Maud of Basingstoke."

She had come to Winchester a few years ago when her father, Prince Malcolm, paid a state visit. She was dark and swarthy and very short in stature. People said that she should have been called dwarf but her mother pleaded with the Seer at her birth and he allowed her to pass for human.

I made a mock punch at him which he parried, laughing. It was good to be back on our old terms. On our way to the stables we gathered loose snow into balls and pelted each other like children.

Once again spring was late. Beyond the walls the fields lay white until mid-April and the thaw when it came seemed partial and uncertain. There were gray skies and a harsh east wind. Farmers, coming into the city on market day for the Spring Fair, complained that the ground was still too hard for planting; they had never known it so bad.

I was too concerned about the new campaign to care much. This year I would not be condemned to look after the baggage train. I was not allowed to be a warrior but I would be a scout, and Edmund with me. We rode our horses far out and practiced the arts of observation on the downland sheep.

The arrangement was that the army of Romsey was to come first to us, to be joined with our army under my father's command; the combined force then moving north against Andover. They arrived late one afternoon and we saw their tents going up in the Contest Field and on open ground around it. That was the place that had been allotted them for a camp. Prince Jeremy had suggested it himself, saying that even if accommodation for his men could be found in the city it was wiser for them to remain outside. Even though our two cities were allies, conflicts might arise in living at such close quarters. My father, who had had similar thoughts, praised this as an example of Jeremy's common sense. There was more to him, he repeated, than his fat foppishness would indicate.

Jeremy, with a handful of his Captains, came in for conference. James came as well. He had not improved in the months since I had last seen him; there was the same mixture of arrogance and sly servility, the same hungry envy for what he saw as our better fortune. Our horses were in better condition than theirs and looked faster, our dwarfs forged better swords.

"And our leather, I suppose," Edmund said to me when I had slipped James's company one day and was telling him all this, "comes from cows with thicker hides. He disgusts me. You say he is to scout for them? Not along with us, I hope?"

"No," I said. "I have made certain of that. The armies part company on the second day. They take a line in advance of us and to the east. The idea is that they draw the Andover army onto them. Then we strike north to the city itself where the south gate will be open."

The plan had been divulged to the Captains so I had felt I could tell it to Edmund; what had been said had been in the Great Hall, not my father's parlor. He now said, brow wrinkled:

"I do not like it. It is not a good way of fighting."

It was what I had said to my father and there were still doubts in my mind. Suppressing them, I said:

"The Spirits approve it."

"Oh, the Spirits . . .!"

There was a noise of someone approaching. We were in the den under the Ruins which bit by bit we had furnished into a sort of comfort, with furniture and rugs taken from unused rooms in the palace and with oil lamps now for lighting. Martin joined us. These days he wore the white of an apprentice Acolyte and his shaved head was covered by a wide-brimmed white hat. I still had not got used to the change in his appearance.

Edmund said: "We can ask the expert for advice. Why is it, Martin, that the Spirits who have in the past told men to fight honorably now urge us to rely on treachery to win our victories?"

Martin said: "No expert. I am not even an Acolyte yet, and will not be for another year."

"All right. But give us an opinion, as one who is planning to spend his life serving these same Spirits. Have they changed their minds? Has the Great Spirit sent out fresh instructions?"

He said it with a smile but Martin did not smile in return. He said, stumbling but in serious fashion:

"Without knowledge one cannot understand things. And knowledge is always limited. What I mean is . . . it is not so much that things change as that they happen in a different way."

Edmund said in astonishment: "I believe they have converted him already."

"I'm not very good at explaining what I mean."

Edmund said: "But you've changed, too, like the Spirits, haven't you? You take it more seriously."

"Do I?" His expression showed reluctance. "In a way, perhaps."

"Then you've been told things?"

"Not much. Nothing, really."

"Tell us. We'll judge."

Martin looked more and more unhappy. I said:

"He is bound by oaths and you know it. He must not tell the secrets of the craft and we must not ask him."

"Let him speak for himself," Edmund said. "Do you say so, Martin?"

Martin said uncomfortably: "I've nothing really to say."

Edmund looked at him curiously. "You believe in the Spirits now—is that it?"

"Yes," he said. But it sounded as though the word was being dragged out of him. "I believe in them."

We left the city the day before we were to march on Andover and camped in the fields on the far side of the road from the Romsey army. The reason for this was that Prince Jeremy had invited our men to join his at supper on the eve of our campaign together. He said that although it had been wise to keep the two forces from mixing inside the city, it was also wise that they should meet and feast moderately together before setting out. In this way they would get to know and have confidence in each other. My father was more dubious about this than he had been about the earlier suggestion but agreed that it could do no harm. The feasting, he pointed out, would need to be moderate, particularly as far as drinking went, since we were to ride next morning.

When we went over I, of course, found myself saddled again with James. He took me down the lines, denigrating even his men, which I thought unpardonable: they were less stout than ours, he said, but then they did not live so well. I ignored that and asked him about something else which struck me as odd: they had bowmen with them, at least a hundred. I could not understand what they were doing with an army in the field. Bowmen were part of the garrison, a defensive force. James said:

"An idea of my father's." He shook his head. "It probably won't work."

"I still don't see . . . Even if they could come up with a troop of horse, the horsemen would gallop out of range before they could do any real damage."

"It's something to do with a scheme for luring the enemy into an ambush where the bowmen would shoot them down. As I say, it will very likely prove useless."

"But meanwhile your own walls at Romsey are undefended."

He gave a high laugh. "The women can toss slop buckets down on anyone who attacks. Apart from that, they can take their chance. The bowmen are defending the one Romsey skin that is precious. In my father's eyes, at any rate."

I said in annoyance: "I do not think that is true, unless it is your own skin you mean. Your father is concerned for you more than himself; and more, perhaps, than you deserve."

"What does he deserve? Does a weak man deserve anything?"

"A son owes a duty."

"You can say that," he said bitterly, "with a father such as yours." He looked at me with hatred for once showing instead of the usual ingratiating affability. "You can respect your father."

It was not worth responding to the remark. We went on down the lines and he showed me the horses, drawing attention to their weak points. But he came back to the subject just before we parted. He said:

"You will grieve, I suppose, when your father dies?"

"Yes, but I do not expect to do so for a long time to come."

"It could happen in this campaign. He fights in the van, doesn't he, not from behind like the Prince of Romsey?"

"But fights well. It would take a good man to unhorse him."

He laughed, but it was more a titter, mirthless.

"Good warriors have been brought down before now by cunning lesser ones."

I said nothing, but left him.

The feasting was moderate as Jeremy had promised: extremely moderate. The meat was barely enough to go round and the ale, which for some unfathomable reason they called the Strong, was thin and sour compared with what our men were used to. There was some grumbling but our Sergeants controlled it well and got the men back to their own lines fairly early on the promise of a measure of decent ale there. It was not a particularly auspicious start to a joint expedition, but it could have been worse: there had been no fighting or even quarreling.

My father did not come back with the rest of us. Jeremy asked him to stay the night in his tent, an ornate affair four times the size of my father's own and lined with silk: in this respect, at least, James could not bemoan Romsey's poverty. Jeremy said he wanted to have a final private discussion about the campaign. I think my father thought he was nervous and needed reassuring. At any rate, he agreed to stay.

In our camp there was for some time a buzz of noise, part of the excitement which always attends the first few days in the field. Gradually it died away as the night drew on. I myself lay awake for a long time, turning restlessly despite my weariness. It was not the hardness of the ground which caused this—I had grown accustomed to hard living the previous summer—but a fit, for which I could find no cause, of my old melancholy. When I did sleep I had bad dreams: I could not remember what they had been but twice I woke in fear, sweating despite the chill of the night.

After that I slept heavily, exhausted. Edmund had to shake me into consciousness. I blinked up at him, and asked:

"What is it?"

"They've gone . . ."

"Gone? Who? What do you mean—gone?"

I was aware of a hum of talk and shouts outside; it had an anxious disturbed note like that of a hive broached by a clumsy beekeeper.

"The Romsey army. They have left camp in the night."

"My father . . .?"

"I don't know."

I pulled clothes on and ran out, Edmund with me, to find the Captains. They too were agitated and most of them talking at once. They paid me no attention. It was some time before I could piece things together. The Romsey tents were still there, with their baggage train and heavy gear. But there was no sign of men or horses. Except for six men. My father's bodyguards lay outside the Prince of Romsey's tent with their throats slit. Of my father there was no sign.

Blaine said, above the others: "They cannot have got far. We can be up with them before they reach home."

"If they are heading for home."

That was a Captain called Greene, a man who did not say much but usually talked sense.

"Where else?" Blaine asked.

"They have left their tents and gear," Greene said. "Would they do that unless they were sure of exchanging them for something better?" There was a silence in which I heard a rooster crowing distantly through the dawn air. "The plan was to take one of the Andover gates by treachery. There are gates nearer than Andover."

As he spoke we knew it was true. Blaine cursed but quietly, not with his usual bluster. Then Greene called one of the Sergeants to form a troop. The Captains rode with it and I also. I was not invited but no one told me I must not. We rode, in near silence, along the road to the East Gate, past the abandoned Romsey camp.

Light was beginning to come into the sky behind our backs but it was difficult to see much. We had almost reached the East Gate before Blaine, with an oath, halted his horse and pointed upward. The pole above the gate carried a flag, and its colors were not the blue and gold of Winchester but the yellow and black of Romsey. We stared at it. While we were doing so the air hissed and a man cried out; his horse reared and dragged him away, an arrow in his throat. We knew now why Jeremy had brought his bowmen.

Blaine called a retreat. We went, but not before I had seen something else, stuck on a spear over the gate, flapped over by Romsey's flag. It was a man's head. At that distance and in the half light one could not see the face but there was no doubt whose it was. It wore the spiked helmet of the Prince of Winchester.

NINE

Bold Peter

"When I get him," Blaine said, "I will have him scourged each day for a week and in between he will lie naked in a salt bed. Then I will have his chest opened and his ribs pulled outward, slowly, till he looks like a bloody eagle. I will . . ."

"Get him first," Harding said drily. "Then you can show us how inventive you are."

They were talking about the Sergeant in charge of the East Gate who, it was well nigh certain, had let the Romsey army in. He was a man called Gray who, people now remembered, had fought well against Alton and Petersfield. He had been rewarded with gold but had not thought the reward enough. He had hoped to be ennobled, having an ambitious wife. But ennoblements were rare, however good the fighting, and his wife was disliked and despised by the city's Ladies.

"Robert should not have trusted him with command of a gate," Blaine said. "He should have been out in the field with us."

Greene said: "His wife is with child and the last she had was polymuf. She expects to bear within a month. That was why he asked leave to stay behind, and was granted it. It could not be known that he was treacherous."

"A Prince should know these things," Blaine said, "or guard against them."

"If he was at fault," Harding said, "he was the first to pay for it."

We were at our camp, in the conference tent. It was a cold morning and rain had begun to fall, rattling harshly against the canvas. I stood in a corner, unregarded. My skin was clammy with a cold sweat, my mind turned in useless narrow circles, fastening again and again on the sight which, above all, I would have shut out forever from my mind. But it would not be dismissed; the harder I tried the faster and more vividly it winged back.

Greene said: "Being deceived by Jeremy was the greater error. But, by the Great, what a fox he is! Promising Robert that he would give him Andover and using that same trick to take Winchester . . . I would not have thought, with his scents and silks, that he had the guts to try it."

Blaine said bitterly: "That's what comes of making a man like that our Prince. You need breeding to be a judge of character."

"Would you have judged Jeremy better?"

"I never liked him."

"Nor did Robert," Greene said. "A Prince does not have

to like his allies. And the Spirits favored the scheme."

"Curse the Spirits!" Blaine burst out. "I would have liked to see Ezzard's head beside his on the gate. They have betrayed us worse than Jeremy."

There was a silence. After a moment, Blaine blustered on:

"There are Spirits and Spirits. Remember what Marinet used to say?" He had been Seer before Ezzard, and better liked, though Ezzard had been more feared. "There are Spirits whose delight is to lead men into mischief, which the Great One permits as a means of testing, and of humbling those who puff themselves up beyond their merits. They start with gifts and promises but they end with destruction. Was it not those Spirits who led our ancestors blindfolded to the Disaster? And have they not done the same with Robert? Can anyone deny it?"

Harding said: "It may be." He was a small, wiry, sharp man, who talked less than Blaine but could usually silence him. "Perhaps we shall have leisure to talk of it during the long winter evenings. But there are more pressing needs. Jeremy has our city. We must decide what we should do."

"He has ours but his own is ill guarded." It was Charles who spoke, the brother of Edmund, son of Prince Stephen. "If we rode hard for Romsey we might take it and have something to bargain with. His bowmen are here."

Greene said: "Not all his bowmen, I'll wager. If he is fox enough to plan this he will have made his defenses sure at home."

"We could try at least."

There was no enthusiasm for the suggestion. An army whose own city was in enemy hands attacking a stronghold . . . it was not a picture to inspire much hope. A Captain called Ripon said:

"Well enough for you. But we have womenfolk at hostage."

"I also," Charles said. "My mother and my sister."

"Mothers and sisters!" Ripon said. "We have wives and daughters."

During Blaine's abuse of my father, the cold shock which had stunned me had been giving way to anger. It was against Blaine in the first place, but I knew he was not worth it. It was Jeremy who had tricked my father and slaughtered him while a guest in his tent.

I said: "Why do we wait?"

Their eyes turned to me. Blaine said, sneering:

"The brat has counsel for us. Speak up, then, you that were to be Prince of Princes. What would you have us do?"

"Not stand here talking!" I saw my father's head again with the Romsey flag slow-flapping over it and the memory maddened me. "We should attack the walls at once and force them! We should have done so right away instead of letting two or three arrows drive us back."

Blaine laughed. "Attack the walls . . . he's a merry youngster! Those walls which Stephen built up year after year till they were the highest and strongest in the land. Go and do it yourself, lad—you need no help from us. The Spirits will give you wings or maybe tumble the walls down for you. If you don't know how to summon them, go to the head that sits on the East Gate and ask him to do it for you."

I went at him blindly. He smiled and cuffed me, knocking me to the ground. He had great strength and all of it was in the blow: his anger drove him, too. Dazed, I heard Harding say:

"We waste our time discussing fantasies. It makes no sense to do anything until we have heard from Jeremy. I do not think he will keep us waiting long."

The herald came an hour later, alone and unarmed, riding a black horse with the white cloth of truce trailing soaked, from its reins. He was brought to the conference tent and stood there, wiping rain from his face with his sleeve.

His name was Grant and he was the best liked of the Captains who had accompanied Jeremy when he came to the Christmas Feast. He had seemed a decent and sensible man, level-eyed and level-headed. He did not look as though he enjoyed his errand. Harding said:

"Greetings, Captain. You will not expect much by way of welcome, seeing what brings you here. Do you have a message from your master?"

"Yes," Grant said, "I have a message. He bids you return in peace to your city and your homes."

Harding had been nominated to speak for the rest. He said: "On what conditions?"

"Sergeants and men will be admitted twenty at a time,

and unarmed. They will be imprisoned under guard, but only until the peace settlement has been made. Captains may keep their swords."

"Why? To save our honor?" Grant nodded. "Is there any honor left after treachery such as yours?"

"It is not treachery to forestall treachery. By taking your city our Prince only defended his own."

"Do you say that we are weasels like you—that we planned to attack Romsey, not Andover? If so, every man here knows you lie, and knows therefore what trust to put in any new promises fat Jeremy makes."

"Not this year, maybe, but our Prince is far-sighted. Robert took Petersfield last summer and, against all the customs of war, kept it. He was to rule over Andover as well. Where would this have stopped? Was it not said that his son was to be Prince of Princes, ruler of every city in the land? Would Romsey, lying so close to Winchester, have been allowed to escape? Had you been Captains of Romsey you would have had good cause to fear the future. Can any man here deny it?"

Harding said: "And therefore we are to accept the rule of your Prince instead, and of that whining, sniggering son of his after?"

"No. Our Prince restores the ancient customs. There will be tribute, of course, but you may keep your city, choosing a proper Prince to rule it. Petersfield, too, will be free. The Prince of Romsey does not wish to govern lands outside his own."

Harding did not reply at once. I looked at the faces of the other Captains and found them thoughtful.

Harding asked: "Is that the sum of his demands?"

Grant shrugged. "There will be small things to be discussed. But you get your own city back, and your own Prince. He will promise that."

I said: "As he promised to fight with us against Andover? As he promised my father friendship?"

Grant glanced at me but did not answer. He looked unhappy, as though what I said had brought him back from the safe neutral ground of arguing policy to the closer, harsher truth of hospitality polluted, confidence betrayed. It was Blaine who said:

"Shut up, boy. Keep silence in the presence of your elders and betters. You are here on sufferance, so do not try our patience."

Grant asked: "What answer do you give me to take back to my Prince?"

Harding said: "Tell him we have received his message. We will consider it, and send him word."

Grant bowed. "I will take that news to him. I hope we may soon drink together at the peace feast."

No one answered him. Blaine said something that sounded like a curse, almost under his breath. Grant left the tent in silence, and we heard the jangle of harness as he mounted his horse and rode away.

The Captains wrangled until dinner, finding no common agreement. Some, like Blaine, were for defying Jeremy, but could put up no suggestions of how to do this, or none that carried weight. Others, fewer in number, argued that we must accept his terms, having no choice. I managed to hold my tongue, though with difficulty. It was true what Blaine had said: I was there on sufferance and there was nothing to stop them putting me out. It was more important to know what was happening than to offer opinions which in any case I knew would be treated with contempt.

Dinner was brought to us at the middle of the day. It was hard tack: soup, salt beef, hard biscuit, a small measure of ale. The army had its rations but in no great abundance. We had looked to living off Andover's land. It would not make us popular to raid our own farmers. The rain had set in heavily and ran in rivulets between the tents; the horses stamped miserably at their tethers and the men were full of gloom and grousing. A raw breeze blew chilly from the city whose walls, once our safeguard, now mocked us.

When talk resumed, there was a change in atmosphere. Harding talked more. After the herald left he had listened for the most part, sounding out the others for their views. Now, with patience and skill, he was trying to influence the Captains to his own way of thinking. And that way, it became more and more clear, favored acceptance of Jeremy's offer.

"And if we do," Blaine shouted angrily, "what guarantee do we have with our men disarmed and guarded? He will leave us our swords, will he? And what good are twenty swords against an army? Even that fool of a boy"—his small eyes darted in my direction—"could see that. Jeremy's promises are worth nothing. Nothing! Is he to swear by the Spirits? When he has already defied them?"

"He has defied the Spirits that led Robert Perry astray," Harding said. "So he is favored by other Spirits who are more powerful. Or else Robert was abandoned and it is all a game. You said yourself that there are Spirits and Spirits. But if he swears by the Great Spirit Himself, I do not think he will break his oath; or if he does that his men will follow him."

There was a murmur of agreement: an oath made on the Great Spirit must be binding. Harding said:

"We must not deceive ourselves: he has us in the hollow of his hand. He speaks softly now because he hopes for peace, on his own terms. But if we defy him I would give nothing for the safety of our womenfolk. And the men will not be easy with the thought of a Romsey army walking their streets unchecked. If we choose to fight I would not be sure that they would follow us. And how can we fight? Blaine has said it: the walls Stephen built are the strongest in the land. We would only break our bones on them."

He spoke calmly and reasonably, therefore persuasively. I saw some nod their heads, among them Greene. Harding went on:

"If we surrender now we do not surrender for all time. He lets us keep our swords, but I do not think any of us will forget what happened this morning. There will be a time to fight again. Not for the sake of a Prince whose ambition is well ended, but for our honor."

"He may bind us in a treaty of peace," Greene said.

"No doubt he will. And we will keep it as long as they do. But who has ever known a treaty of peace that the other side could say they kept in everything? And if they break it, we are free."

He was winning them, and not to his plan of action only. His aim, I saw, was deeper. The city lacked a Prince and he was advancing his claim. Blaine had shown himself rash and the Captains, smarting from being tricked, wanted a man of guile and caution. They had chosen Harding to speak to Jeremy's herald. If they followed him now they would acclaim him even before the men of Romsey rode away.

He had been cunning, too, after stressing the inevitability of surrender, in raising hopes of revenge. Ripon said:

"They will break it! And by the Great, when they do . . ."

Other voices rose, on the same note of resentment but also with new assurance. Then one said, strongly:

"Wait!"

It was Peter, my cousin. He had not spoken in all the previous talk. Looking at him I had thought him stunned, perhaps even more than I was, by what had happened. But he spoke now with strength and confidence. On that single word they listened to him.

He said: "I can show you how to win back the city and not lose a man."

Blaine began to say something but stopped. Harding said:

"This one has gone mad. We know what blood runs in his veins."

Ignoring him, Peter said to the other Captains:

"Or would you rather bend your knees to Jeremy, pay him gold, watch him drive off Winchester cattle and load his carts with your women's jewels?"

"If you are not mad," Greene said, "tell us how."

"I have conditions first."

"You name conditions!" Blaine said. "A Perry, commoner born, naming conditions to us . . .!"

He stared at Blaine. "Yes, I name conditions."

His voice was level, without anger but with certainty. Greene said:

"If this is a jest, Perry, you may find the laughter cut short. Say it quickly."

"There are two," Peter said. "The first is that a ransom is paid, but not to Romsey. We will pay gold to the Christians so that they can build a church to their god."

There was a confusion of protest, laughter, incredulity. I heard Harding's voice: "Mad, as I said. Do you want more proof?" Peter let them run on for some moments. Then he said, and they went quiet as he spoke:

"This will be done because it is through the Christians that the city will be regained."

"How else?" cried Blaine. "We had forgotten those warriors of ours. I can see them, driving the Romsey men down the High Street with their crosses!"

Peter ignored him. He said:

"You know that in Winchester men despise them, but do not harm them. It is not so everywhere. In some cities they are harried by Seers who have them tortured or killed for refusing to worship the Spirits. And even where they are safe for the moment they have no confidence that the safety will last. If Ezzard does not persecute them, the next Seer of Winchester might. So they take their precautions."

He paused before going on. He had all their attention, even Blaine's.

"I have considered this all day. As you will guess, I have it from my wife. She was bound to keep the secret, but told me. Her trust in me binds me also. If I break it, as I think I must, then I demand a tribute for her god, to turn away his wrath. Do I get this from you?"

Harding stared at him with cold, appraising eyes.

Greene said: "If it is worth it, you get it."

"It is worth it. A tunnel that goes under Stephen's great walls. Cramped and dirty, but men can crawl through it. It was the way of escape for the Christians and can be a way in for men who will take the North Gate and open it to our army. I know where it starts. Will you give them gold and the right to build their church?"

"By the Great," Greene said, "I will! And I do not think any will refuse."

I heard voices speak approval and none opposing.

Peter said: "That is one condition."

Blaine asked: "And the other?"

"My father is dead. He died by treachery, murdered by his host. Jeremy dies for this. There will be no ransom for the Prince of Romsey."

They roared assent, and he put a hand up to stop them.

"That is not the condition. I did not think any of you would let him live. My father was a great Prince. His

Spirit requires more than just revenge; it needs his own blood to follow him in power, his son in the Great Hall."

I saw them look at me. Blaine said:

"He is a boy, too young to govern himself, let alone a city like ours."

Peter looked at me, too, and smiled. I saw the smile but could not read what lay behind it. He said:

"You mistake me, Blaine. My father had two sons. I was first born. I claim his place."

There was silence again and his unwavering, confident gaze went round their faces. Then Greene broke out:

"Do as you say, Perry, and you have my voice!"

The rest followed. Even Blaine and Harding were forced to an assent. Blaine gave it grudgingly but Harding showed no emotion in his voice.

The rain stopped toward evening. The sky above the city was painted in scarlet and orange. Clouds hung huge over the walls, first red then purple, at last black against a deep-blue sky. Occasionally one saw a head silhouetted above the battlements, one of Romsey's men. It was not until full darkness came that the army marched, quietly and by a circuitous path, to take up its position outside the North Gate.

I watched with Edmund. Peter, with two other Captains, one of them Greene, and a band of picked men, had left for the hut, a broken-down shack thought to be abandoned years before, under whose floor the tunnel started. They would come out into the house of the Priest, as the leader of the Christians was called, near the North Gate and from there it would be easy to fall on the Romsey men defending that gate from behind. Our army waited for the sign, a torch flourished in the gateway, which would tell them the way was open.

Time dragged by—minutes, hours it seemed. We did not speak much. We were each occupied with our own thoughts. Mine were confused and bitter. This morning the thought of seeing Jeremy's head set up in place of my father's would have been a joy to override anything. It was so no longer. The blackness of despair was back in my mind, the sense that all was useless: one could not live without hope, but always hope betrayed.

It was cold even though the rain had stopped. I started to shiver but I think it came more from melancholy than from the night air. I tried to stop it, not wanting Edmund to notice, but could not. He shifted beside me, and said:

"Luke."

"Yes."

"When this is over, what do you plan to do?"

"Don't know."

I answered shortly so that he would not hear my teeth chatter. He said:

"If you thought of leaving the city, going north perhaps, I would go with you."

I did not answer and he did not speak again. I was too bitter and wretched to realize what he was offering: that having weathered his own grief and disappointment he would still go into exile with me as a companion to me in mine. Later I understood. Friendship meant much to him, more than it could ever do to me.

We waited and my limbs shook. I set my jaw until it, my neck, my whole body ached with the strain. Then the light shone ahead, the dull tramp of feet went past us, and soon, following after the army, we heard the distant sounds of the struggle. Not for long. We had the advantage of surprise and our men were fighting in their own streets. Inside half an hour the last of Romsey's warriors had laid down his arms. Inside an hour fat Jeremy's head topped the palace gate.

I went back that night with Edmund to the house in Salt Street, though I did not sleep. Next morning, after breakfast, I slipped away without a word and went to the palace. Because he would have insisted on coming with me I said nothing to Edmund. Whatever I faced was mine, mine only, and I would face it alone.

I stood for a while in the crowd that stared at Jeremy's head. They were in a festive mood, many drunk already, and from time to time they roared for their Prince, Peter, to come and show himself. I saw Christians there and men slapping them on the back as comrades while they looked dazed and disbelieving. A player was singing a song made up for the occasion:

> Under the walls bold Peter came—
> Took the gate with a torch of flame—
> And so made good his father's shame . . .

A new roar drowned it as Peter came out on the balcony. I slipped away and in at a side door. I passed polymuf servants; some of them bobbed to me but others did not. Two soldiers stared at me and one laughed behind my back. I went to my room and waited for whatever was to happen.

Martin found me there, staring blindly out of the window at wet roofs under a gray sky. He said: "Luke," and I turned.

"Ezzard wants you."

"He will find me here."

"The risk is too great."

"Poor Ezzard."

"For you both. You must come."

"No must," I said. "I have had enough of must from Fate itself."

"Remember what the High Seers said: that you have a mission and when the time comes you must obey. You promised it."

"I never told you that."

"But I know."

"And you still believe that nonsense?"

"More than ever."

There was passion in his thin face. The tricks by which Ezzard had won him over must have been good ones. I argued for a while but he had more conviction than I, who was waiting for I knew not what except that it could not be good. I went with him, through the palace and out into the street. Someone jeered after us. He did not lead me

toward the Seance Hall but along a side street. We stopped
at a house near a tavern and, after a quick look round, he
drew me in.

Ezzard was waiting in a room upstairs. He looked more
white and gaunt than ever. He said:

"Well done, Martin. Leave us now." As the door closed,
he added: "We must get you out of here, Luke, and
quickly."

I said: "I came for one thing, sire. To curse the Spirits
who led my father to his death, and the Seer who spoke
for them."

He showed no anger. In a quiet voice, he said:

"Curse if you will, but do as I say. Your life is not worth
a halfpenny here. Even if Peter does not order it, someone
will have you killed, thinking to please him. You were
named heir and Prince of Princes. Alive, you challenge his
power. Things may be different later but these are days of
doubt and murder. Leaving Peter out of it, there are
enough who would rather see one Perry left than two. Your
only hope is in flight."

"I will not flee."

"Listen, boy. You are a fool but not a complete fool or
you would not have been chosen. Even though he is dead,
would you do your father's will?"

"If I knew it. Are you to tell me? But for you he would
be living still."

"Did he fear death?" I hesitated. "You know better. He
thirsted for it. If the Spirits guided the assassins' knives he
thanked them for it with his last breath. Is this not true?"

I was silent. He said: "Your father lived to do his duty and prepare for your succession."

"My succession!" I laughed. "As Prince of Princes."

"Yes. And the prophecy lives while you do. The Captains know that. So does your father's Spirit. Can you deny it? If you will not ask me what he would have wished, consult your memory of him. It is fresh still."

In my mind I saw him, sitting in his armchair in front of the painting of my mother. His eyes were on me. Was everything a waste, all hope and effort, did everything shatter and fail? I could not think otherwise but he had, and perhaps had died with that belief outweighing the pain and betrayal. I owed him something.

I asked: "Where would you have me go?"

"To the Sanctuary. Where else?"

I nodded. "As you wish, then, sire."

TEN

The Prince
in Waiting

I left the city of my birth in a shameful fashion. Ezzard
found rags for me to wear and fixed a cloth hump on my
back so that I looked like a polymuf. He for his part put on
women's clothes, a tattered gray cloak and a pointed hat,
and walked slowly as though hobbled by old age. But the
disguise was good. I saw several people who would have
known me but they paid us no attention except one, a son
of the kite-maker in West Street, who slashed at me with
his stick when I was not quick enough in getting into the
gutter to give him room.

We went out by the East Gate because there was more
traffic through this than the North. Some of the soldiers
on guard were drunk and singing. I looked back when we
were outside, half dreading that my father's head would

still be spiked above it, but it had been taken down. I did not look back after that.

The baggage train of the Romsey army had already been taken into the city. The Contest Field was empty but scuffed and muddied by their occupation. I thought of my own day of glory there and of that last charge against Edmund which had won me the jeweled sword. It hung in my room in the palace now: I wondered who would get it.

I had asked Ezzard if I could say good-by to Edmund but had not been surprised that he refused. I had not even seen Martin again after he left me with the Seer. Already I might have been missed from the palace and word gone out to find me. I wondered what Edmund would think when it was known, as it must be soon enough, that Ezzard and I were both gone. That, having refused his offer to flee with me, I had run for aid to the Spirits, still hoping they would win me my inheritance? I would have liked to be able to tell him it was not so. But it did not really matter. Nothing mattered. It started to rain again. That didn't matter either.

When we were well clear of the city we halted in the shelter of a clump of trees and I was able to get rid of my hump and both of us to dress ourselves in the more ordinary clothes we had brought in a bundle carried under my arm. We looked like farm workers now, or maybe vagrants. Before resuming our journey we ate there—a hunk of bread and cheese with an onion—and slaked our thirst at a stream nearby.

We had simple food to last us three days. It was five and twenty miles to the Sanctuary on crows' wings, probably half as far again by road and at least twice the distance by the circuitous route which we must follow to give a wide berth to any place where we might be sought. The pigeons, if they were not already flying, would soon be out with orders for us to be arrested; and we could not be sure that this applied only in Winchester's lands. The Princes of both Andover and Salisbury might be asked to trace the fugitives and might think themselves well advised to do so, as a favor to the man who had nailed Jeremy's head on his palace gate.

We tramped steadily westward, using roads or tracks but taking cover when anyone came our way and keeping well away from villages. We went in silence, speaking only on necessary matters. I was not sorry for this. It was not that I was contented with my own thoughts: in fact they followed a treadmill of anger, resentment, jealousy and despair. Certain moments and events came back again and again, and seemed each time to leave me still more numb. My father's head on the spike above the East Gate . . . the Captains giving their voice to Peter while the rain slashed against the walls of the conference tent . . . the crowd in front of the palace roaring for him . . . But I knew no conversation, with Ezzard or anyone else, would drive away those images or my feeling of black hopelessness. I suffered them better in silence.

The road to Stockbridge was over high ground but Stockbridge itself lay in the valley of the Test River. We left the road some miles from the town and went north. In the early evening we could look down and see the distant town and the river running through. I remembered we must cross it and wondered what Ezzard proposed. Even from here, a quarter of a mile away, it looked turbulent, swollen with the waters of the spring thaw. Swim it? And spend the night freezing in soaked clothes? I asked Ezzard.

"You see the high-road that runs this side of it?" I nodded. "Two miles north of here it crosses the river."

We made our way across a field to the high-road. At this point it was not, in fact, very high, only a few feet above the level of the surrounding land. We walked beside it until it was necessary to go on it to cross the river. Dusk was heavy by now and we saw no one. The road was carried over the river by a metal bridge. Ezzard said suddenly:

"Have you ever wondered, Luke, why our ancestors built the high-roads?"

There were two near Winchester, forming an ellipse that enclosed the city. I shook my head.

"No, sire."

"Your friend Martin has done so."

"He has strange thoughts." I realized that this could seem a criticism and endanger him, he being an Acolyte, and added: "I do not mean impious ones."

Ezzard did not seem to notice it. He went on:

"Or why they are made as they are? We call them high-roads because sometimes they stand high above the fields. But in other places, as at Shawford, they run in valleys cut out of the hills. Have you ever thought of this?"

I said I had not. He stooped and pointed to where one of the thick timbers, which were still found in places on the high-roads though mostly they had been taken for winter fuel, was raised a little above the dirt.

"Or what these were for?"

Near one end the beam carried a metal socket that looked as though it in turn had supported something, a rail perhaps, running transversely across it. I said:

"I suppose they were to do with machines."

I felt guilt in even speaking the word in the presence of the Seer, but he had asked strange questions. He said:

"And these machines—were they so much weaker than a horse that they could only travel on level ground; and therefore the high-roads had to be raised up or brought down, not taking the shape of the country through which they passed?"

I said: "I do not know, sire."

I was embarrassed. Such speculations surely were forbidden. It might be different for the Seers, who served the Spirits, but I had no right to think them.

He did not speak again for a time. Then he said:

"You must prepare yourself for strange things at the Sanctuary, Luke."

"Yes, sire."

Of course there must be strange things—I knew that. Like a Seance going on all the time, perhaps: darkness with lights and bells and the sonorous voices of the Spirits. Ezzard said:

"Strange things to learn as well as to see. Your mind

may be amazed by some of them." He paused but I said nothing. "You are strong in many ways, but curiosity is not one. I do not suppose it is necessary. But it would have been better if we had had more time to prepare you."

I did not understand what he meant but was not sufficiently interested to want to find out. I was tired and hungry, my feet sore from walking all day. I was glad when we came to one of the broken-down huts which you find here and there on the high-roads and Ezzard called a halt.

We slept the second night in a barn. The straw from last year's threshing made a warm bed—it had been cold in the hut with no blanket—but I slept badly. A rat ran over my arm and lying awake I heard them scuffling. I have a dread and loathing of these beasts from the time when I was a child of two or three and an old cat of ours, a hunter, brought one back and laid it on my pillow; and I awoke and in the dim glow of the night light saw its dead face close to mine. I got up and went outside. The night was almost clear, bright stars everywhere, and the fires of the Burning Lands brighter than I had ever seen them. We were nearer to them now, of course. I huddled up against the side of the barn, staring at them while I went the same dreary round of memory and anger and melancholy. In the end, despite my cramped position and the cold, I fell asleep. I was wakened by Ezzard's voice calling my name in the thin dawn light. I answered and he came to me. There was relief in his face. He said:

"I thought I had lost you, Luke."

"I could not sleep in there."

I would not speak of the rats, and my fear, to him. He said:

"Tonight you will sleep in a bed."

I nodded. "I will be glad of it, sire."

But I was not glad when, at the end of the afternoon, he pointed and I saw the Stones of the Sanctuary ahead of us. They stood like jagged teeth on the skyline; tiny but, being miles away still, having the promise of enormity. The promise or the threat. I had made this journey as a duty to my father's memory, not thinking of its end. There had been vague thoughts of the High Seers, of Seances, but nothing concrete, nothing, really, that meant anything. Those distant pillars were real, and foreboding. They were surrounded by empty downland, cropped only by rabbits. No man would go near, no shepherd graze his flocks in their shadow. It was the place of the High Seers, dread and holy, and that dread touched me, making me want to turn back toward the world of men. I would rather have taken my chance with Peter and his Captains than go forward. But I had come so far that I must go on to the end. And again I would not show my fear to Ezzard.

It was a long walk toward them. The sun, sinking, had come out from behind clouds and cast shadows from the Stones that stretched tenuous fingers in our direction. I could see them more clearly. They roughly formed a circle, great jagged-hewn wedges many times the height of a man and broad in proportion. They were set apart from each other but some were linked by other immense stones resting on top and between them.

Inside there was nothing but the rabbit-cropped grass. I felt a new and different alarm. Could this emptiness be the Sanctuary? I had expected a huge building, a castle perhaps. Where did the High Seers live? There was only grass and the great time-weathered stones. Did one walk through a doorway in one, into the Spirits' world? Or climb an invisible ladder to a stronghold in the clouds?

We crossed a shallow ditch and the stones loomed over us. We passed between two of them, scored by the wind and rain not of years, it seemed, but centuries. Within the outer ring were other stones, some standing and some fallen. Near the center, beside one of these, was a sort of mushroom, made of stone but whiter and less pitted than the bigger ones. It was only a few feet high. Ezzard went to it and put his hand underneath, feeling for something. I stood beside him, telling my limbs not to tremble. We waited in silence, for half a minute perhaps. And then the stone mushroom spoke:

"Who comes?"

The Seer bent his head toward the mushroom.

"Ezzard, with the Prince in Waiting."

I do not know what I expected to happen: thunder and lighting, perhaps, a chariot of fire appearing out of the sky, a solid rainbow leading to a magic land. Instead there was a creaking sound and the ground on the other side of the mushroom moved, splitting and opening. There was not darkness revealed but light, a whiter, brighter light than I had ever seen, the steps leading down.

Ezzard said: "Come, Luke."

I hesitated. They were ordinary steps but they terrified me. And the light . . . the light of the Spirits? I remembered all the events they had set in motion. Maybe they had helped me to win the jeweled sword and my father to the Princedom. But after that . . . my mother slain, my aunt executed for her murder, my father's head set up above the East Gate, a thing to be mocked. And I myself driven from the city disguised as a polymuf. The good they had done me was surely outweighed by the evil.

All this was true. What was also true was that at last I faced their stronghold. They could do no more than take my life. It was little enough worth living as it was; if I broke and ran it was worth nothing. I went in front of Ezzard into the hole.

A dozen steps below there was a platform where the staircase turned on itself before descending even farther into the bowels of the earth. Behind me Ezzard stopped and I stopped also. He touched a button set in the wall. There was a whirring sound, followed by the creaking I had heard on the surface, and I saw the gap closing above us, blotting out the sky. I realized then that underneath grass and earth there was metal and this was rising, a trap door to seal the opening at the top of the stairs. I was less alarmed than confused, my mind trying to take in what could not be denied and yet was impossible. The light, I saw, came from long tubes of glass. Ezzard touched another button and more of them flashed into radiance, lighting the stairs below.

"Ezzard!" I cried. "These lights . . ."

He looked at me. I could scarcely bring myself to say it, but it was not possible to be silent.

"They are not the lights of the Spirits . . . and the trap door, that is not the work of Spirits either. These are machines!"

"Yes," he said. "I told you there would be strange things to learn."

I sat at supper with Ezzard and the High Seers. They wore no cloaks but simple clothes—trousers and shirt—as Ezzard did also; and except for Ezzard their heads were not cropped but carried a normal covering of hair. On the senior of the three, who had come to Winchester, it was sparse and white with age but the big one had a heavy thatch of black. And he did not, I noticed, eat with the sparrowlike delicacy he had shown at my father's banquet but heartily, as a man who enjoys his food. Like the shaved heads and the cloaks, that had been done for show.

It was strange, too, to hear them speak in easy, unmeasured voices—to speak and even laugh. They were ordinary men, and relief and disappointment were at war in me, realizing this. I was silent, putting no questions and answering briefly the questions put to me. There were not many of these: I guessed they were letting me get used to things by degrees, accustom my mind gradually to its shock. I learned their names: the little white-haired man was called Lanark, the big dark one Murphy.

When supper was over each took his own plate to the kitchen where they were stacked in a machine that washed them: one could hear the rush of water behind the closed door. There seemed to be no servants—I supposed because there were no polymufs. One of the men operated another machine that moved across the floor with a whining sound, sucking crumbs and dust into itself. The others led the way into a large room with many chairs and couches. The walls had been painted with scenes of landscape framed by pillars—a forest glade, a garden, a view of rocks and sea, and on the fourth the streets of a city, with men and women, children, a dog scratching itself in the dust. They were reminders to men who lived like moles underground of what the world was like.

We took seats. Lanark said:

"Now, Luke, what would you like to know?"

There were so many things that it was hard to think of one. I said after a moment:

"The machines—what makes them go?"

"Electricity."

"What is that?"

"A force. It is hard to explain. Something which is invisible but which can be used."

"Invisible? Like the Spirits?"

He smiled. "No."

I said, with daring: "Do the Spirits exist?"

I still half expected to be condemned for blasphemy. But Lanark said:

"If they do they have not shown themselves to us."

"The Seances . . . the lights and sounds . . ."

"Are trickery, to keep the power of the Seers over men's minds."

"The prophecies . . ."

"Prophecies often fulfill themselves because expectation brings its own results. Where they fail"—he shrugged— "they can usually be explained away."

I shook my head. My mind was fuzzed with doubts and uncertainty. I said:

"I don't understand."

Lanark said: "I know it isn't easy. Best, perhaps, to take things from the beginning. You know what is said of the Disaster?"

"That our ancestors were given powers by Spirits who led them on and then, in the end, destroyed them, casting down their cities and making the earth itself spew flame."

"It has some truth in it. Our ancestors did have great powers, they built cities in which a thousand Winchesters could be dropped and lost, they had machines in which they could fly through the air—around the world in less than a day—or see things as they happened thousands of miles away. They traveled to the distant moon. Then came the Disaster.

"The strange thing was that many men had expected it, though not in the form in which it happened. Because among the machines were machines of war: by pressing a button a man could destroy from half a world away a city so large that Winchester by comparison is but a hamlet. It was thought that sooner or later these powers of destruction would be unleashed and the world driven back to barbarism if it were not destroyed entirely. Men feared this possibility. Later the anticipation was confused with the reality."

I asked: "What did happen?"

"The earth itself rebelled. Except that that is a wrong way of putting it: the earth is inanimate, without will or mind. But it has life, of a sort. It can change, and change violently. Men knew that in the past, the incredibly distant past before man himself existed, there had been convulsions of the earth in which vast lands were crumpled like parchment, mountains thrust into the sky, volcanoes belched fire and molten rock. There were still a few volcanoes, now and then an earthquake. Occasionally a town was shattered, a few hundred people killed. These were freaks of nature, unexpected, soon forgotten.

"Then the earth's fires, smoldering for a thousand million years, broke loose again. We do not know why. Some think it was to do with the sun, which just before showed puzzling signs—strange bursts of radiation accompanied by dark spots across its face. At any rate, the earth shook and heaved and everywhere men's cities tumbled and men died in their ruins. The worst of it did not last long, days rather than weeks, but it was enough to destroy the world of cities and machines. Those who survived roamed the shattered countryside and fought one another for what food there was.

"Gradually they came together again. They built houses to protect them from the weather—of wood, not stone, and designed as far as possible to withstand the earthquakes which still continued, though more and more rarely. They returned to their old places, at least to the villages and the small cities. Not to the large ones which were left as rubble. They did as they had done in the past—grew crops, raised cattle, traded and practiced crafts and fought. But they would have no truck with machines, identifying them with their forefathers' ancient pride and the reckoning which had followed. Anyone found dabbling with machines was killed, for fear of bringing down fresh destruction.

"They had many religions in the old days. One was concerned with what were supposed to be the Spirits of the dead and this now spread like wildfire. Seance Halls were built and in them, in the dark, the Spirits were supposed to talk to men, to guide and counsel them.

"But there were a few men, a handful, who were not content with this, who knew that machines were not evil in themselves and in fact could help us back to civilization. They dared not defy the legends—those who did were torn to pieces by the mob—but they could use them. They became Seers and took over the Seance Halls. They preached anathema to machines but preserved the knowledge of them, all the time looking for likely recruits."

"Martin . . .," I said.

"Yes, such as Martin. And at certain places, called Sanctuaries and so holy that no one would come near them, they built machines and worked with them. Here, and elsewhere. Do you understand now?"

"Partly," I said. "But not why I was brought here. To work with the machines?"

Lanark smiled. "We would sooner have brought Martin. For you we have different plans, very different. Do you remember what I told you when we met in Winchester?"

"That the Spirits had a mission for me to perform."

"There are no Spirits, that we know of, but there is a mission. I said that men recovered from the Disaster but only some men, in a few favored places. These lands are one such. Outside there are deserts and desolation, and monstrous beasts. There are also savages. They multiply fast and hunger drives them against the civilized lands. The winters have grown longer and harder because the sun's rays are weakened by dust thrown into the sky by the volcanoes. The cities themselves are beginning to feel the pinch, with farmers growing poorer crops and raising fewer beasts. Four years ago Taunton fell. Dorchester was besieged all last summer and the barbarians are at the walls again. And when a city falls to those enemies there are no ransoms—only plunder and murder, followed by fire and ruin.

"We have spoken with men in far parts of the world who share our aim of restoring civilization. Not through the pigeons; we have machines that can do this as our ancestors did. At one time there were many voices, but they grew fewer. For a year we have had no answer to our calls.

"Men's loyalties were narrowed by the Disaster. The cities, when they were rebuilt, warred fiercely against one another, each remaining sovereign and separate, violently hostile to the rest. There have been similar times in man's history. But the only hope of resisting the savages is for the cities to join together; individually they have no hope."

I said: "So when Ezzard told my father the Spirits wished him to keep Petersfield, against all custom . . ."

"It was part of the plan. There had to be one city that would dominate and unite the others. Winchester was best for this. It is well placed, at the center of the civilized lands, and rich; and there is a memory in men's minds that once, hundreds of years ago, a great Prince ruled from there.

"But having chosen the city we needed a Prince. Stephen was no good to us, a timid, unambitious man. His son, Edmund, might have served. If there had not been someone better we should have had to use him. But Ezzard found you and when, against great odds, you won the prize at the Contest, our choice was made certain."

"But it was only by accident that I was in the Contest at all! If Matthew had not fallen ill with a fever . . ."

"No accident," Lanark said. "It takes no great art to raise a fever."

I remembered meeting Ezzard in the High Street and how he had told me to make the most of my skating since it might be my last winter for it. I said:

"And everything after that . . . my father becoming

Prince, the two crowns of light at the Seance . . . all these were contrived?"

"Your father's election needed skill. The crowns of light were a simple trick."

"But the machine that burst and burst the walls of Petersfield—you could not have known that would happen!"

Lanark smiled. "Could we not? When one understands something of gunpowder it is not too difficult to make a cannon blow up. The Seer of Petersfield saw to it."

Disbelief still lingered; and disappointment. I had thought I accepted the loss of a destiny predicted by the Spirits, but a part of me still balked. I said:

"At the Seance of the Crowns . . . there was a farmer who complained that he had paid gold to the Seer to protect his lambs but lost them all the same. And the Spirit of his grandfather's father charged him with breaking the laws by rearing polybeasts. He could not deny it. So surely it was a Spirit that spoke, and spoke truth?"

Ezzard answered: "There is not a farmer in the land who has not been guilty of the same sin. Who is to tell how many horns a cow had when it is carcass meat? I was on safe ground in condemning him."

"And my father—he told me he obeyed your orders because it was through you he heard my mother's voice after she was dead. Was this a trick also?"

"In part, but he heard her voice. Through another machine of our ancestors. Words are trapped on something like a ribbon, which can be cut and put together again so that the words make a message that one chooses."

A new and terrible thought came. "My mother's death . . ."

Lanark shook his head. "That was not our doing. We cannot control everything as was shown by Jeremy's capture of the city. We made use of it to help bind your father to us. But it was a blow all the same, a bitter blow. It turned your half brother against you. Because of that Ezzard had to flee with you and bring you here."

"Your plan had failed already when Jeremy took the city."

"Not failed. We could have worked on him. He would have let you be Prince in your father's place, thinking you a boy and powerless."

I said angrily: "Do you think I would have taken it from his bloody hands?"

"If Ezzard had shown you a hope of revenge at the end, you would. You are a good hater."

I knew it was true. I said:

"But it was all for nothing. Peter has the city and I am here in exile. So you have failed after all."

Lanark shook his head. "We have lost one battle, but there will be more. While you live you are still the Prince in Waiting."

"An empty promise," I said, "from Spirits that do not exist."

"Not just that," Lanark said. "A hope also, the hope of living men."

In the weeks that followed I learned many things. About polymufs, for instance. The word came from an older one, meaning of many shapes. Such freaks of nature had increased after the Disaster and it was thought they were caused by strange radiations from the sun, probably the same which were believed to have reawakened the earth's deep fires. Some, like the dwarfs, bred true, but most did not. In civilized lands men had done their best to extirpate all the freaks among animals, but mothers would not let their babies be killed. So they were allowed to live, the dwarfs as a race apart, the polymufs as servants to normal men. In the savage countries, beyond the Burning Lands, there was no control and misshapenness ran riot.

I learned about the Seers. This was not the only nor the most important Sanctuary. There was another in the ruins of the great-city which had been called London. They told me it had stretched over more than six hundred square miles and eight million people had lived in it: figures so great that one could not imagine the reality. The Seers had found a place, under the rubble, where the wisdom of the ancients was stored in books, and they quarried there for knowledge.

I learned something of that knowledge myself: not much, for my mind was not equipped to grasp it. My purpose, as they told me, was different: to help create the conditions in which knowledge could be brought from hiding and the cities made safe against the sea of barbarism which lapped all round and otherwise must rise and drown them.

And I saw the machines which could do things more marvelous than anything that had been supposed to be done by the Spirits. Machines for seeing and listening at a distance, machines that could propel a carriage ten times faster than a team of horses could pull it, machines that could detect metal under the earth, that could chill meat and keep its sweetness without salting throughout a summer, that could show strange beasts living inside the smallest drop of water . . . a score and more of wonders.

And one day burly Murphy showed me something called an induction furnace. He explained how it worked, through this power that was called electricity. He said:

"It case-hardens steel. You get a hard surface such as no ordinary forge could produce."

I nodded, partly understanding him. He said:

"You left the jeweled sword you won at the Contest behind you, Luke. But do you remember that one day I promised you a sword of the Spirits? Even though there are no Spirits, you will have the sword: we shall make it here and I promise you no sword made by dwarfs will notch it. It will shatter anything that comes against it, if your right hand is strong enough."

"When?" I asked. "When will you make the sword?"

"When it is time."

"But how long will that be? I am tired of living underground, with no wind, no sunlight, no day or night except what we make ourselves."

"We are all tired of it," Murphy said, "but we must wait. There is a moment for striking: too soon or too late and we fail. And if we fail, all hope is gone. You must learn patience, Luke."

He clapped a hand on my shoulder and I nodded unwilling assent. I itched to be on a horse riding through the meadows beneath St. Catherine's Hill, to see the walls of Winchester looming high before me. But he was right, and impatience was at least more easily borne than despair. The time might be long delayed, but the time would come.